While Jessica watched incredulously, Jeremy pulled out a small midnight-blue velvet box from his pocket. He set it on the table between them and opened the lid.

Jessica stared, feeling faint. Her face flushed, then paled, and when she looked up at Jeremy, her pupils were almost black.

"Wha—wha?" was all she could manage.

Inside the velvet box was a ring. It was a gold band with a large blue sapphire as dark as the sky at night. A sparkling diamond glittered brightly on each side of it. It was the ring that Jessica had shown Jeremy almost a month ago at Bibi's, the ring she had said was her favorite. Her engagement ring.

Slowly Jeremy took the ring from the box and slid it onto the third finger of her left hand, which was suddenly ice-cold. Then he clasped her hands in his and said very solemnly, "Jessica, will you marry me? Will you be my wife?"

DOUBLE-CROSSED

Written by
Kate William

Created by
FRANCINE PASCAL

BANTAM BOOKS
NEW YORK · TORONTO · LONDON · SYDNEY · AUCKLAND

RL 6, age 12 and up

DOUBLE-CROSSED

A Bantam Book / October 1994

Sweet Valley High® is a registered trademark of Francine Pascal
Conceived by Francine Pascal
Produced by Daniel Weiss Associates, Inc.
33 West 17th Street
New York, NY 10011
Cover art by Bruce Emmett

ISBN: 0-553-56231-2

Published simultaneously in the United States and Canada

Bantam Books are published by Bantam Books, a division of Bantam
Doubleday Dell Publishing Group, Inc. Its trademark, consisting of the
words "Bantam Books" and the portrayal of a rooster, is Registered in
U.S. Patent and Trademark Office and in other countries. Marca
Registrada. Bantam Books, 1540 Broadway, New York, New York 10036.

PRINTED IN THE UNITED STATES OF AMERICA

OPM   0 9 8 7 6 5 4 3 2 1

To William Benjamin Rubin

Chapter 1

Jessica Wakefield shut her eyes tightly, trying to block out the hazy sunlight filtering through the bedroom curtains. It was far too early to get up, she decided. Rolling over onto her side, she bunched up her pillow and snuggled her head into it.

The next instant she sat bolt upright in bed, her hand to her mouth. A quick glance around the room brought reality crashing down on her: She was at Lila's, in the guest bedroom. It was Sunday morning. Slowly Jessica sank back against the pillows, her long blond hair fanning out behind her head. "Thank heavens yesterday is over," she muttered. "Today's a whole new day. I can start again."

Groaning, she buried herself under the covers, but she couldn't hide from the memories that swirled insistently in her head. Just the day before, Jessica had committed what was perhaps the most outrageous act of all her sixteen years. Which was why she

1

was staying at Lila's: She wasn't ready to face her parents, and she doubted whether her parents were ready to face her. Thinking about it, she flopped onto her other side and rubbed the sleep out of her blue-green eyes. When she opened them again, she was greeted by the sight of a pale-pink dress thrown carelessly onto the back of a chair. Jessica winced. Her bridesmaid dress.

Yesterday she had worn that horrible dress as she walked down a rose-petal-strewn path at Moon Beach, not far from Sweet Valley. A smile plastered insincerely on her face, she had preceded her twin sister, Elizabeth, down the center aisle formed by two groups of white folding chairs that had been set up on the beach for the wedding.

Wedding. Ha! She had stood next to Elizabeth at the front of the gathered crowd as the bride began her slow, almost regal procession. Friends had turned back to smile at the young woman in white while Jessica had gritted her teeth and fidgeted so much that Elizabeth had nudged her with her elbow twice.

Sue Gibbons's dress had been lacy and fitted, with long, sheer sleeves to her wrists. The small incident of Jessica's "accidentally" throwing it under the wheels of a truck didn't seem to have left a mark on it. Tiny white and pink rosebuds were woven into a crown on her chin-length dark hair, and a short veil covered her face. But her beaming smile and glowing, happy eyes as she walked down the aisle on the arm of her stepfather had been apparent to everyone. Especially Jessica.

The beautiful southern-California sun had shone

2

down on the sparkling ocean waves, and the bouquets of roses that surrounded the gathering had released their sweet, heady scent into the morning air. Jessica's eyes had wandered around the area, gazing at the short wooden pier in the distance that she and one of her boyfriends had fallen off once. She couldn't even remember his name now. Several times in her life she had been convinced she was in love—and she knew that what she had had with Sam Woodruff had been deep and real. Since Sam's tragic death in a car accident earlier in the year, Jessica had dated only one other boy—the young English lord Pembroke. And that had lasted only a few weeks.

Sighing, Jessica rolled over in bed again. She examined her nails, which were still polished a frosty pink to match the dress. Her memories drifted back through the summer. . . .

Just a little while ago Jessica had thought her love life was over for good—then she had met the man she knew she was destined to be with for all time. Like a bronze Greek god, he had risen out of the ocean at Sweet Valley's beach. It had been fate. She and Elizabeth had just returned from their terrifying experiences during their apprenticeship at *The London Times*. Elizabeth, and her best friend, Enid, and Jessica and her best friend, Lila, had all gone to the beach for some therapeutic sun and water. She and Lila had gone for a jog along the shore. Then—wham!—Jessica had gotten bonked in the head with a Frisbee. As she had crouched on the sand, rubbing the bruise on her head, her fantasy man had come up, apologizing profusely. His warm hands had examined her injury. Their eyes met, ocean-blue looking into coffee-brown. Her breath had stopped, her heart had slowed its steady beating pulse.

He was a god, her dream come true, someone too gorgeous to be believed and much, much too tempting to be available. As if in a dream they had moved away to sit alone on a covered lounge chair. Barely speaking, they had held hands, had kissed. Then he had jumped up and run off without a word of explanation. She hadn't even known his name.

Since then Jessica had found out who he was. Since then they'd met secretly, stealing forbidden kisses that they both knew were wrong—not only because Jeremy was so much older, but because he was engaged to marry another woman. Sue. Sue Gibbons, the orphaned daughter of Mrs. Wakefield's college roommate Nancy, and the Wakefields' houseguest. And yet Jessica had known it was meant to be, known there was no use fighting it. She was his and he was hers, and she would defy anyone—her parents, her sister, her friends—to be with him.

As she had stood before the wedding party in that hateful pink dress, her small bouquet of pink roses and baby's breath in her hands, she had looked across the aisle and watched the sunlight glint off his tawny golden hair. For just an instant his piercing dark eyes had met hers, and she had twitched, as though shocked by a current of electricity. Glancing away quickly, she was left with a fleeting impression of his broad shoulders, his strong arms that had clasped her against him, his firm chin over his bow tie. She forced herself to look away as the radiant bride came

4

up the aisle, smiling and nodding to people she knew.

Then the love of Jessica's life stepped forward, took the bride's arm in his, and together they stood before the minister. Jessica felt nauseated, faint. Heat was buzzing around her head, the scent of the roses suddenly cloying, sickly sweet. When the man she loved said, "I, Jeremy, take this woman . . . ," Jessica had bit her lip until it bled. She had ignored Elizabeth's startled, concerned look.

Then Jessica had stepped forward, had spoken out, had said the unthinkable in a loud, clear voice.

A gentle tap on her door roused Jessica from her reverie. She sat up in bed and brushed her hair away from her face. "Yes?"

The door opened and Lila walked in. "Good morning, sunshine," she said flippantly. Jessica winced as her friend threw open the curtains, flooding the room with harsh sunlight. Then Lila flopped down onto the overstuffed easy chair that matched the curtains. "And how are we this morning?"

Jessica regarded Lila. They had been best friends, and sometimes best enemies, almost as long as she could remember. In some ways their competition with each other had strengthened their friendship, added spice to it. Lila kept her on her toes.

"I'm not sure how *you* are, but *I* feel totally weird," Jessica admitted.

"You did cause quite a scene yesterday," Lila said, her eyes glowing at the memory. "I've never been to a wedding where someone actually stood up and objected when the minister asked if anyone cared to."

Jessica groaned and sank deeper into the bedcovers. "I don't know what came over me. Jeremy told me that he had to go through with the wedding—especially after we found out that Sue has the same blood disease that killed her mother. But when I saw him take her hand, and it really hit me that they were going to be husband and wife and that I would lose him forever . . ." She trailed a hand across the seam of her pillow, remembering.

"I know how you feel," Lila said sympathetically. "I would have done the same thing if it had been Robby up there marrying someone else." On the same day that Jessica had met Jeremy Randall, Lila had met Robby Goodman, who had been with Jeremy playing Frisbee that afternoon. Lila and Robby had been dating steadily ever since.

"Really?" Jessica asked hopefully.

Lila considered it. "Well, I might not have actually stood up in front of everyone and shouted that the bridegroom was totally in love with me and not his fiancée, but yeah, I would have tried to stop it." A mischievous smile played around her lips.

Jessica groaned again and pulled her pillow over her head. "Oh, Li," came her muffled voice. "How will I ever live this down? How will I ever face anyone again? I've never seen my parents so angry." Jessica sniffled under her pillow. "My mother said she was ashamed of me." Her voice broke. "She actually said she was ashamed I was her daughter. And what are they going to do to me? I'll be grounded forever, I'll never get an allowance again—nothing they can come up with will be bad enough." Sounds of crying escaped from the lump huddled under the covers.

Lila pulled a few tissues from the box on the nightstand and pushed them beneath the pillow. "Now, now, Jessica," she soothed. "It's not so bad. It will all blow over in no time, you'll see. Another week or two, and no one will even remember it happened." She patted the lump through the covers.

Jessica pulled her pillow away, revealing a tear-stained face. "Do you really think so?" She sniffled and blew her nose again.

Lila couldn't lie to her. "Well, no, maybe not," she admitted. "But you did what you had to do for love. Like Romeo and Juliet. How could anyone stay angry about that?"

"I have the feeling my parents can, and they will." Jessica sniffled again. "And I don't even know what Jeremy must think. What if he hates me now? I haven't talked to him since he left after the wedding. Maybe he's totally mortified by what I did. I'm so stupid—such an idiot. I wish I could disappear." Tears began rolling down her cheeks again; then she jumped as the phone on the nightstand rang.

"Maybe it's Robby," Lila said, pouncing on the phone. "I'm supposed to meet him for lunch. Hello?" She listened for a moment, then said, "Sure. Just a minute." Handing the phone to Jessica, she mouthed, "Lover boy."

Jessica sat up in bed and took the phone, feeling a twinge of fear. Lila smiled at her, then turned and left the room, closing the door behind her.

"Hello?" Jessica said hesitantly.

7

"Hey, sweetie," came Jeremy's husky voice.

Jessica melted with happiness. He didn't sound angry. He didn't sound as if he hated her. "Hi," she said.

"How are you, babe? Are you OK?"

Jessica sank back onto her pillow with relief. "I am now that I'm talking to you," she said. "How are you?"

Jeremy sighed. "Well, things are a little messy right now. I'm just trying to straighten everything out."

"I'm sorry," Jessica said softly. "I really screwed it up, huh?"

"No—don't say that. I'm glad you brought the whole wedding to a screeching halt. It was wrong of me to go through with it—to pretend that I felt something for Sue. I mean, I feel bad for her—I want her to be happy." His voice sank lower. "But it's you I love, Jessica. Always."

A blissful smile spread over Jessica's face. This was why she had objected to the wedding yesterday. She had done it all for the love of her life—Jeremy.

"I'm so glad, Jeremy," she breathed. "When can I see you?"

He chuckled. "I'll pick you up at seven—how's that? We'll sneak away to a little restaurant I've heard of, up the coast. It'll be just you and me. OK?"

A pang of disappointment shot through Jessica. She had pictured Jeremy rushing to her side, unable to keep away from her for even one moment now that he was free. . . . How could she ever wait that long? But then she realized there was no hurry—after all, they had the rest of their lives to be together. "That would be great," she agreed happily.

"Why don't we meet in back of the Beach Cafe? That might be better than your picking me up here."

"Good idea. I can't wait to see you."

After she hung up, Jessica luxuriated in bed for a few moments, reliving their conversation. Everything made sense to her now. She and Jeremy were going to be together, no matter what. As for Sue—well, it was too bad. But she would go back to New York soon and get on with her life. That would be the best thing for everyone.

Jessica glanced over at the clock on the nightstand. Eleven thirty. Flinging back the covers, she leaped out of bed and headed toward the bathroom. There was no time to lose. She had only seven and a half hours to get ready for her date with Jeremy.

In the hallway outside Sue's room, Elizabeth Wakefield paused and took a deep breath. She shifted the tray she was holding onto her hip and straightened her shoulders. Then she tapped at the door.

"Come in," came a wavering voice inside. Sue Gibbons had been in Sweet Valley almost a month now. Her mother, Nancy Gibbons, had recently died. When Sue had announced her engagement, Mrs. Wakefield had invited her to California to plan her wedding. She had felt it was the least she could do for the daughter of her college roommate.

Good going, Mom, Elizabeth muttered silently, opening the door.

"Hi, Sue," she said lightly, setting the tray on the nightstand. During her visit Sue had been staying in the room that belonged to Jessica and Elizabeth's older brother, Steven, since he was away at Sweet Valley University. "I've brought you some tea and some more tissues."

"Thanks, Elizabeth," Sue said weakly, taking a tissue. She blew her nose, then pitched the tissue into an already-full wastebasket by the side of the bed.

Elizabeth smiled at her and went to open the curtains. Southern-California sunshine flowed into the room, instantly making it look less gloomy. Then she opened a window. "You need some fresh air and sun," she said matter-of-factly. "It's not good to stay cooped up in the dark like this."

"It doesn't matter," Sue said listlessly. She glanced up at Elizabeth, winced, and looked away again.

Elizabeth frowned. Because she and Jessica were identical twins, Elizabeth would, of course, remind Sue of Jessica. They both had long golden-blond hair and blue-green eyes. They were the same height, five six, and had the same slim, athletic build. They even had identical dimples in their left cheeks. But looks were the only similarities they shared. From the time Elizabeth had been born, four minutes before Jessica, she had been the more reliable twin, the more reasonable one. She was studious at school and made good grades. *The Oracle*, Sweet Valley High's newspaper, depended on her writing and editing. Her boyfriend, Todd, and she had gone out steadily for as long as anyone could remember. Fun loving but not reckless, sensitive but not stuck-up, Elizabeth preferred the company of a few good friends to a buzzing, noisy crowd.

Jessica, on the other hand, had always enjoyed

being at the center of every wild party, the leader of any crazy prank, the flame that drew helpless boys like moths. School was merely a place to socialize with her friends and show off how cute she looked in her cheerleader's uniform.

Elizabeth sighed. There was nothing she could do about her outward resemblance to Jessica, the cause of Sue's heartache. "Sue," she suggested, "why don't you get up now and take a nice hot shower? That always makes *me* feel better."

Sue sniffled. "I think I just feel too bad for anything to help right now, Elizabeth. But thanks." Sue wriggled farther underneath her covers, pulling them up so that only her face and one hand holding a tissue stuck out. "The only thing I really want," she said, her voice quivering, "is for Jeremy to call me and say the whole thing was a mistake, it didn't happen." Sue started crying again. "And that he still wants to m-m-marry me!" A fresh torrent of sobs broke free, and Sue cried harder than Elizabeth had ever seen anyone cry. Quickly she came to sit beside Sue, putting her arm around the other girl's shoulders.

Jessica, you have really done it now. And Jeremy! What a loser. Engaged to one woman and fooling around behind her back with a high-school student. What a creep. And poor Sue, left at the altar and living with the weight of a life-threatening disease hanging over her.

"There, there, Sue." Elizabeth went to get a wet washcloth from the bathroom. Sue took it and wiped her tears away. Her hair was tangled and messy, her face flushed and shiny, and her nose swollen and red.

Elizabeth thought she had never seen anyone so miserable in her life.

"You know, Elizabeth," Sue said after she had calmed down a little. "At first I was so happy when Aunt Alice asked me to come to Sweet Valley for my wedding. But now I wish I had never come." Her voice shook.

"I don't blame you," Elizabeth said sincerely. "I just wish there was something I could do to help."

Sue managed a watery smile. "Thanks, but I just want to go to sleep now and not wake up for twenty years. If ever." Her face crumpled, and she began to cry again. Elizabeth sat by her helplessly. *She has to stop crying—she'll make herself sick. Poor Sue—what if this whole disaster causes her disease to come out of remission? It's just a romance for Jeremy and Jessica, but this could mean life or death for Sue.*

Frowning, Jessica held up the black tank dress and regarded herself critically in the mirror. "I don't know. What do you think?"

Lila, perched on the bed, cocked her head to one side. "I like it. It's sophisticated, sexy, classy. Perfect."

Jessica whirled around, clutching the dress to her chest. "Thanks, Li," she said. "What would I do without you?"

"I guess you'd have to float around ecstatically by yourself," Lila said with a grin.

Jessica laughed. "Got a date with an angel . . ." she sang, heading toward the bathroom. "Li, where's your curling iron?"

*   *   *

Elizabeth thumped down the stairs despondently. What a mess. Of all the stupid, selfish, un-thought-out things Jessica had ever done, this one really took the cake. Sue was practically a basket case, Elizabeth's parents were furious, and just about all of Sweet Valley was going to be buzzing with this awful gossip for who knew how long to come.

At the bottom of the stairs she headed for the kitchen.

"Well, OK. I think we have to consider it. She's just gone too far this time. I feel like she's out of control. It really worries me."

Elizabeth paused at the sound of her father's voice. She glanced at her watch, surprised to see it was only just after lunchtime.

"Daddy? I thought you were going in to work today?"

Mr. and Mrs. Wakefield were sitting at the butcher-block kitchen table, mugs of coffee in front of them.

"Come in, Elizabeth. Sit down," her mother instructed her seriously. "We need to talk to you. It's about Jessica."

Gulping, Elizabeth sat down. She knew that what Jessica had done was completely out of line. But she was afraid to hear what her parents were planning to do about it.

"Jessica, phone," Lila called. "It's Elizabeth."

Jessica sighed, looking in the mirror. She was right in the middle of arranging her hair in a loose bun on top of her head. Of course she'd have to face

13

Elizabeth sometime, but she was hoping it wouldn't be for another day or two. Still, she grabbed the cordless phone that Lila handed her.

"Liz? Hi." Jessica knew Elizabeth was appalled at what had happened yesterday and no doubt blamed it all on Jessica. But if she would just think about it for a minute, she would realize that if Jeremy had truly been determined to go through with his sham of a wedding, he wouldn't have jilted Sue just because of one little thing Jessica said.

Jessica knew she had to tread carefully if she was to keep Elizabeth from turning against her completely. Elizabeth had known that Jessica was secretly seeing Jeremy behind Sue's back, even as Sue and Elizabeth were planning the wedding, and she had thought it was awful.

"Liz, I don't know what to say," Jessica said, stalling for time. "I don't know what happened to me yesterday. All of a sudden I felt overwhelmed by emotion. . . ."

"For another woman's fiancé," Elizabeth said.

"Sue's hardly a woman, Liz. She's barely two years older than us. She just graduated from high school last year. She's not even old enough to drink." Jessica twirled the phone cord around her finger.

Elizabeth sighed. "Are you sure you want to be involved with a man who's willing to be unfaithful to his fiancée?"

Jessica frowned. "He wouldn't do that to me," she said finally, but the fire had gone out of her voice. She hated it when Elizabeth found her weak spots. Which she always did. "Anyway, when is Sue taking

14

off?" Jessica couldn't stay at Lila's forever, and she couldn't bear the thought of Sue hanging around the Wakefields' house any longer. Every time she saw her, Jessica would feel both angry and guilty, and she didn't need it.

"Number one, Sue is not taking off," Elizabeth told her. "Mom has suggested that Sue stay here for a while until she gets back on her feet, and Sue agreed."

"Well, if she's going to be there, I'm not," Jessica said decisively. "I'm staying here at Lila's."

There were a few moments of silence. "Jess—are you still going to see Jeremy?" Elizabeth sounded troubled.

Jessica sank down onto the chair. She felt tired— she knew there was still quite a battle ahead of her. Jeremy had walked out of the wedding, but the war wasn't won yet. "Yes, I am," she told her sister softly. "I can't help it, Liz. I feel like I can't breathe if I'm not with him."

Elizabeth took a deep breath. "In that case I think I better tell you something. Mom and Dad are thinking about sending you to boarding school. Out of state. They think you're totally out of control, and they're so angry and embarrassed about the wedding, Dad was even talking about bringing Jeremy up on charges of contributing to the delinquency of a minor."

Jessica snorted in disbelief, but an icicle of fear gripped her heart. "That's ludicrous," she snapped bravely. "I'm not a delinquent and Dad knows it. I'm sure this whole boarding-school threat is just that—a threat. No way would they do it. Don't let them get to you—I'm certainly not."

Elizabeth was silent on her end.

"Now, if you'll excuse me," Jessica said, trying to remain calm, "I've got to finish my hair."

Chapter 2

"Hi, Robby. Sorry I'm late. I got held up patting Jessica's hand."

Robby stood with a smile, and Lila gave her boyfriend a kiss on the cheek.

"You're always worth waiting for," Robby said, pulling out her chair.

Lila smiled at him, at his handsome face, his shiny black hair and piercing blue eyes. The past month had been heaven on earth, ever since she and Robby had gotten together. Who ever would have thought that two such different people could make each other so happy? Lila was the daughter of one of the wealthiest families in Sweet Valley and had lived her whole life surrounded by pampering luxury. Robby was practically penniless and had delayed going to college for a year while he tried to work on his art. But Lila had never been so comfortable with a guy, so content.

When they had first met, Robby had pretended to be as wealthy as Lila, because he wanted to impress her. And Lila had really enjoyed the fact that he seemed to come from a background similar to hers. When she had found out the truth—that the fancy house, the fancy car, the flashy clothes belonged to his father's employer—she had broken up with him. But after several miserable days without him, missing him and wishing he was with her, she had decided to accept him the way he was: charming, attractive, talented, dirt-poor, and crazy about her. Since then their relationship just seemed to get better every day.

"Well?" Lila said eagerly. "Have you seen Jeremy? What did he say?"

Robby handed her a menu and edged his seat closer. "Not a lot, actually. He sort of blustered around, putting on a stiff front. All I could get him to say was that Sue and Jessica were both great girls, and he had a lot of thinking to do."

"Hmmm." Lila scanned the menu. "The Spanish omelet sounds good." She closed the menu with a snap, then leaned forward. "You mean he didn't say that he was dumping Sue forever and definitely committing to Jessica?"

Robby made a rueful face. "Not exactly."

Lila's brown eyes went wide. "Whoa. I wonder what he's going to tell Jessica tonight."

"Oh, don't get me wrong," Robby said quickly. "I think he's crazy about Jessica. It's just that he did have this big commitment to Sue. He can't turn it off like tap water."

Lila nodded thoughtfully, then sighed. "What a

18

mess. I feel sorry for everyone involved. I just hope he doesn't break Jessica's heart."

Robby leaned over and took her hand. "Aren't you glad you don't have to worry about that?" he asked teasingly.

"What—you breaking my heart?"

Robby nodded. "You know I would never do that." He brushed his lips against her fingers, and Lila felt a thrill run down her spine.

"I know you wouldn't, sweetie," Lila cooed. Then her eyes hardened. "Because if you did, I would hunt you down like a dog in the street. You can run, but you can't hide."

Robby threw back his head and laughed, and Lila started giggling also. Then the waiter came to take their order.

They had taken only a few bites when Lila suddenly said, "Oh, I forgot! The plot has thickened a bit. Elizabeth called Jessica right as I was leaving, and you'll never guess what's going on." She scooted her chair foward. "Jessica's parents are thinking about sending her away to boarding school. In Washington State."

"You're kidding! Because of the wedding fiasco?"

"Uh-huh. Elizabeth told Jessica that their folks think she's out of control—they want her to be in a more structured environment, so she can think about what kind of person she wants to be. They think she's gone too far this time and hurt too many people. Plus, they think if she's far away from Jeremy for a while, they'll forget about each other." She wrinkled her brow. "They don't know Jessica."

"Wow." Robby pulled his salad toward him and took a few bites. "It seems kind of harsh. A boarding school in a different state. What did Jessica say?"

"When I left, she was trying not to cry, because she didn't want her eyes to be red for her date tonight with Jeremy. But she's pretty upset."

"What a mess. Well, if I hear anything from Jeremy, I'll let you know, OK?"

"Uh-huh. It would all be a lot easier if she were eighteen and could just run off with Jeremy now."

Robby's eyes crinkled. "That's the trouble with you young things: You're jailbait."

Lila slapped his arm playfully. "You're barely two years older than I am. But Jeremy's seven years older. I sure hope they know what they're doing."

"Enough about them!" Robby broke in, leaning closer to Lila.

"I have some exciting news of my own. A local gallery wants to show some of my paintings."

"Robby! That's fabulous! I'm so proud of you." Lila leaned over and gave him a kiss. "At last someone has recognized the fact that you're the most talented artist Sweet Valley has ever seen."

Robby grinned. "I don't know about that, but yeah, I'm pretty excited about it. This could be the break I need. It's the Drake Gallery, downtown. They show a lot of new young artists."

Lila wiggled with excitement. "Is it a one-man show? Will there be a fancy opening night?"

Laughing, Robby said, "No. It's a group show—a bunch of unknown artists. But there will be an opening-night party. And, Lila, I wanted to ask you: Do you think your parents would let me show that painting I did of you?"

Lila's eyes sparkled. "They wouldn't dare say no. It's one of the best things you've ever done."

"I had a great model," Robby said.

Smiling, Lila gazed into his eyes. She couldn't wait for the opening-night party. It was time people realized what a great artist Robby was. "So what are the terms of the gallery's contract?" she asked. "I mean, if you don't mind telling me."

"I don't mind. I have no secrets from you—"

Lila nodded impatiently. "Uh-huh. Are they giving you a good deal?"

Robby told her about the contract the gallery had given him, and the terms they had offered should they sell any of his works. "I'm going to sign it today and drop it by."

Frowning, Lila took a sip of her iced tea. "I don't know, Robby. Maybe you should have one of Daddy's lawyers look it over. Those terms don't sound very fair to me."

Robby waved his hand dismissively. "The way I see it, that's not even important. At this point I just want the exposure. I'll worry about the terms for the next show—if there is one."

Lila looked at Robby. "Robby, how can you say that? Of course this contract is important. The way you start determines the way things will be from now on. You can't let them walk all over you like this. Give me the contract and let me have Daddy read it. He can decide whether to show it to his lawyers or not."

Robby smiled and brushed his hand along Lila's

cheekbone. "Thank you for caring, beautiful. It means a lot to me. But I'll be OK. Don't worry about it. Worry about what you're going to wear to the opening-night party instead."

Taking Robby's hand and holding it, Lila said, "Robby, just because I'm female and younger than you doesn't mean that all I have to worry about is my wardrobe. I haven't lived with my father for sixteen years without picking up a little business sense. And I *know* you can get a better deal from the gallery."

"But, Lila, getting a better deal isn't what my life is about. All I care about is my art. And you."

"Look, just because you're an artist doesn't mean you shouldn't have a handle on the business end of things too. You need to know about it so you can take care of yourself."

"Lila, I appreciate your interest, but let's not waste this gorgeous day worrying about details like that. Let's just enjoy being together. Now, where should we go next? What do you feel like doing?"

Lila bit her lip and looked down at her plate, trying to keep her irritation in check. Finally she swallowed and said, "How about a nice drive up the coast? It's so beautiful outside. You feel like doing that?"

A broad smile lit Robby's face. "Yeah, that sounds great. Let's go." He threw down some bills and pulled out Lila's chair for her.

Fine, Lila thought, standing up and straightening her white linen dress. *But you haven't heard the last of this, Robby Goodman.*

❖   ❖   ❖

22

"Everyone is going to be talking about Jessica," Enid Rollins said, adjusting her sunglasses on her nose.

Elizabeth rolled her eyes at her best friend. They were lying on lounge chairs by the pool in Elizabeth's backyard late Sunday afternoon. "I know. What can I say? Jessica is like a force of nature: uncontrollable."

Enid had been at the wedding the day before and so knew all the gory details. "Is she really in love with this guy? I mean, he's good-looking—gorgeous, in fact. But is she serious? And is he serious about her?"

Elizabeth shut her magazine and took a sip of lemonade. "I don't know about him, but I think she's pretty serious. I haven't seen her like this since Sam." Elizabeth couldn't hide her automatic flinch when she said his name. Indirectly, she'd been responsible for his death. He'd been a great guy, and she still missed him.

"What are you going to do?" Enid asked. She took a long sip of her diet soda. "I mean, he's so much older. You don't think they're going to—"

"Enid! For heaven's sake. I think she may have one functioning brain cell left in her head." Elizabeth put her lemonade down with a thump.

"I was going to say 'elope,'" Enid said mischievously.

Elizabeth started laughing. "Seriously, though. There's nothing I can do—at least not to Jessica. This is one scrape I'm not interested in cleaning up. All I can do is try to help out here, try to comfort Sue somehow. Unfortunately, every time she looks at me, she sees Jessica."

"Can't get around that," Enid said reasonably.

Elizabeth sighed. "No, I guess not."

Enid's eyes widened. "Speak of the devil," she murmured in a low voice.

Elizabeth looked up to see Sue pushing open the sliding glass doors leading to the patio. She was wearing a black one-piece bathing suit and carrying a towel.

"Sue, come join us," Elizabeth offered immediately. "Soak up some of this California sun."

"Hi, Sue," Enid said. "Let me help you set up a lounge chair. It's important to be at an exact ninety-degree angle to the sun for even tanning." She got up and began to pull a chair closer to hers.

Sue managed a wan smile. "Thanks, guys. I think I'll swim for a while, then come sit with you." At the edge of the pool she dropped her towel, then dived into the water headfirst.

Elizabeth and Enid shrugged at each other and watched Sue start churning up the pool's blue water in a fast-paced crawl. "She's been crying ever since the wedding broke up yesterday," Elizabeth whispered. "In the middle of the night I got up for something to drink, and when I walked by Steven's room, I heard her still crying. I'm really worried about her."

Enid nodded sympathetically. "I guess only time will help her feel better. After all, it was just yesterday that her whole world fell apart."

Elizabeth made a grimace. "Yeah, and we have my dear sister to thank for that. Not to mention her horrible partner in crime. Why can't she see what a phony Jeremy is?"

Sue continued to swim lap after lap, not pausing to rest. After several minutes Elizabeth began to feel worried.

"What is she doing?" she whispered to Enid. "It's like she's obsessed."

Enid shrugged, a concerned look on her face.

Finally, after countless laps, Sue wearily climbed the steps of the pool. She was breathing hard and her face was flushed from exertion. She picked up her towel, then flopped onto the lounge chair Enid had pulled closer.

"Sue, you should be careful not to overdo it," Elizabeth cautioned gently. "Just rest and take things easy for a while." She got up to pour the older girl a glass of lemonade.

"Thanks, Elizabeth," Sue said, drying her hair. "But I felt like I needed to get rid of some energy—wear myself out." She stared dully off into the distance. "Just to keep my mind off things." She sighed deeply. "Oh God, what am I going to do now?" she said, a despondent and hopeless note in her voice. "I had my whole life planned—now I don't know what I'll be doing tomorrow." Her voice trembled, and she wiped her eyes with the corner of her beach towel. "All of a sudden nothing makes sense. For a little while everything in my life was just the way it should be. Now nothing is. And the man I thought I was going to spend the rest of my life with . . ." Her voice broke off and a little sob escaped. Turning away from them, she wiped her eyes with her towel, then took a sip of lemonade. She breathed deeply a few times and turned back to them.

"I'm sorry," she said. "I didn't mean to come out here and ruin your afternoon. But every time I think I've put it out of my mind, it all crashes back down on me."

"We understand," Elizabeth said sympathetically. "Don't worry about it. We're your friends, and we just want to help any way we can."

Sue smiled tremulously. "It's just that—well, I guess my mom was right about Jeremy after all."

"What do you mean?" Elizabeth asked.

"Mom and Jeremy never got along—not from the first moment they met." Sue shook her head. "It was instant dislike, although Jeremy never said anything bad about her. But she really didn't like him—she didn't trust him. I never knew why—I thought she was being totally unreasonable. But maybe she saw something in him that I didn't. Something that told her he would let me down."

Sue leaned back in her chair and closed her eyes.

"But you never saw anything that would make you doubt Jeremy?" Enid asked.

With her eyes still shut Sue shook her head. "No. I guess love really was blind, in this case. Not even after he and Jessica started going places together, movies and shopping and stuff, did I suspect they were anything but friends. But my mom didn't trust him. She kept suggesting that I date other guys too, and said I was too young to settle down with one person. But I wouldn't listen."

Enid made *tsk*ing sounds. "I dated someone once that my mom didn't like. It can be really difficult, because you want to be with that person, but you hate displeasing your parents, too."

Sue nodded. "Yeah. I started meeting Jeremy outside the house, so that he and Mom never saw each other. She didn't actually forbid me to see him, but I knew she was unhappy about it. Then we got engaged." Sue opened her eyes, looking off into the distance. "I was so happy. I was sure Mom would be happy too, when she saw how thrilled I was. But it just upset her more. Finally, when she realized I was going to go through with it, that I really loved Jeremy and was going to choose him over her, she gave me an ultimatum."

Elizabeth saw Sue's face pale as she recalled the painful memories. "What did she do?"

Sue frowned. "She cut me out of her will." She looked over at Enid and Elizabeth. "That's why the wedding budget was so small—because Jeremy was paying for it himself. But I kept forgetting that we didn't have a lot of money to spend—I kept wanting it to be bigger and better." She made a disparaging face. "Maybe that's what turned Jeremy off. I don't know. Anyway, when Mom told me I was out of the will, I was worried about what Jeremy would think. He knew that I was supposed to get a lot of money, and Mom was already sick by then."

"A lot of money?" Elizabeth asked. It was the first she'd heard of it. She'd always thought Jeremy was the one with the money.

"But Jeremy just laughed and kissed me, and said that he already had everything he needed or wanted, because he had me." Sue's eyes teared up again. "He said it would be fun to start from scratch together, without my inheritance."

"Inheritance?" Enid's eyes were round.

"Yeah." Sue smiled wryly. "My mom's family founded MealQuick, those frozen dinners you see in the grocery store."

Elizabeth stared at Sue, then put her hand under her chin and pushed her jaw closed. "You're kidding! I've eaten a ton of them. They're great! I can't believe you've never mentioned this. Does Mom know?"

Sue let out an almost natural-sounding giggle. "She might not. My mom was kind of embarrassed about it. I mean, frozen dinners. It's kind of silly. But anyway, they've made a fortune for us. So you can see why being cut out of Mom's will actually meant something pretty big. When Jeremy said he didn't care about the money, it made me love him even more, if that's possible." For a moment her eyes looked dreamy; then they hardened again. "But now of course I'm wondering if Jeremy really was just after my money, like Mom thought. And here I am, and I don't have either Jeremy or the money. It serves me right for being so stupid. I wish I had listened to her." Suddenly Sue bent over and started weeping again. "I wish I could have told her just once before she died that she had been right about him, and that I was sorry!" Sue's voice was drowned by the sounds of her sobs.

Elizabeth jumped up and went over to Sue, putting her arms around her shoulders and gently rocking her back and forth.

"Shh, shh, it's all right," she murmured. "It's all

right. Your mom knows you loved her. I'm sure she understood."

"Oh God, Mom, I'm so sorry," Sue said through her tears.

Elizabeth met Enid's eyes over Sue's back. Enid's eyes were welling up with tears too.

"But I guess it doesn't matter," Sue sobbed. "None of it matters anymore."

"Shh, shh," Elizabeth said. "Don't say that. It'll all work out. You'll see." But in her heart she wasn't sure if that was true. This new information about Nancy Gibbons suspecting Jeremy of fortune hunting was very telling. Suppose for a moment it was true—what did that say about Jeremy's relationship with Jessica? Although the hot afternoon sun was beating down on them, Elizabeth felt a sudden cold twinge of fear.

Chapter 3

"Yo, Wilkins."

Todd looked up to see Winston Egbert waving at him from across the parking lot. "Hey, Winston. I didn't know you came here." It was late Sunday afternoon, and Todd had just parked his car in the small downtown lot next to his barber's.

Winston nodded. "I've always gotten my hair cut at Rigoberto's. Once I tried that place in the mall, and they did an awful job."

"Yeah. A haircut can be a tricky thing," Todd acknowledged as they headed across the sidewalk to the old-fashioned barbershop. "My dad started taking me here when I was little, but I don't know—I think I might be ready for a change. I've had the same haircut since I was in second grade."

Winston laughed. "Maria has been trying to get me to grow my hair longer. She says I'd look good with a ponytail." Maria Santelli was Winston's girlfriend.

Todd pushed open the door to Rigoberto's. "What did you tell her?"

"Over my dead body, of course."

Todd laughed, and they sat down to wait their turns.

"So who usually cuts your hair?" Todd asked.

"Rigoberto. But I see he has a new guy working here."

"Uh-huh." Todd looked around the sunny barbershop, with its white-painted walls and large mirrors. "Oh, look, the new guy's open. You want to try him?"

Winston shook his head. "Nah. I guess I'll stay with Rigoberto. You go ahead."

"So I guess you won't be here for dinner," Lila said, watching Jessica do her face in front of the makeup mirror. Lila was lying on her stomach on her double bed, her shoes kicked off and her feet swinging around in the air.

"No. Jeremy and I will grab a bite somewhere." Jessica thoughtfully lined her eyes with blue eyeliner, making them seem even bluer and more mysterious. "I hope it's okay with your mom. I don't want to cause any trouble for her."

"No, it's okay with her. Your mom told her the conditions for your staying here: home by ten o'clock on weeknights, homework done, and you have to let my mom know where you're going. But dinner doesn't matter. She'll just tell Susan to set one less place."

Jessica shot her a smile in the mirror. "Thanks, Li. I can't tell you how much I appreciate being able to stay here. If I had to stay at my house, everyone would be taking bets on who'd kill me first: my parents or Sue."

Lila laughed. "I'm sure Sue has considered it. I would have, if you had taken that hunk away from me." She sat up and tossed her long brown hair over one shoulder. "But then, I never would have let him get away."

Jessica rolled her eyes tolerantly, smiling at her friend. "Oh, yeah, that's you. Ms. Femme Fatale Fowler."

Lila smirked. "Believe it. Are you taking the Triumph?"

Jessica nodded. "If that's okay."

"Sure. I don't need it." Lila sighed. "I might actually stay home tonight. Robby's busy and I don't feel like going out without him."

Jessica made a big production of gasping and grabbing her heart. She turned around in Lila's swivel chair to stare at her. "What have you done with the real Lila?" she demanded.

In Rigoberto's Todd was regarding himself in the mirror. "Hey, I like it." Todd smiled at his reflection.

"It's different, huh?" The young hairstylist seemed pleased. "See, it's the latest look. I just got back from New York, and all the guys there have this cut. It's kind of urban, kind of dangerous looking, am I right?"

"You're right," Todd said. He ran his hand through his hair. It was very short, almost shaved on the sides and back, but much longer on top, and sort of flopping forward into his eyes. He had seen the same haircut on a guy in a music video.

"I think it's you, man," the stylist said proudly. "Not many guys can carry off this look, but you can. It was made for you. Brings out your cheekbones, makes you look older, kind of reckless. Know what I mean?"

"Yeah, I do. Reckless. It's great. Thanks." Todd stood up, still examining himself in the mirror, and paid the guy, adding a generous tip. He felt excited and happy; he looked so different, so unlike himself. It was like a beginning—the beginning of a whole new Todd.

"Oh. My. God." Winston stared at himself in the mirror in front of his barber's chair. "I don't believe this is happening."

"What's the matter, Wilson?" Rigoberto asked cheerfully. "You no like? Same as always, hah?"

"Winston. But it's not the same as always, Rigoberto. I don't part my hair in the middle like this. And I don't slick it down with gel. This doesn't look anything like me." The more Winston looked at his hair, the more upset he got. This was the very definition of hair disaster. How could this have happened? And he had a date with Maria tonight.

"Winton, I'm not happy if you're not happy." Rigoberto looked sad, almost forlorn. "How long I been cutting you hair? Long time. How long I been cutting hair? Very long time. Never has someone not been happy. Now you say you not happy."

"Winston. It's just that I wanted my usual cut. This isn't it."

Rigoberto pulled on his mustache. "What you want me to do, Wallace? You want maybe I take little more off?" He thumbed the blade of his scissors.

"No!" Winston jumped out of his chair and tore off his sheet. "Let me go home and mess with it. How much do I owe you?"

Rigoberto took the money, then said, "If you not happy in one day, two days, you come back, I cut you hair for free, hah, Walt?"

"Winston!" He shot out the door of the barbershop, his hands over his head.

Todd was waiting outside, and when he saw his friend, he grinned. "I see we both have new looks."

"I don't want to talk about it," Winston muttered. Then he looked closely at Todd's haircut. "Hey, that looks great. See, that's what I wanted. Something different but cool. Not different but geeky."

Todd laughed. "Just go home and wash all the stuff out. It'll look fine."

"Yeah, right," Winston muttered bitterly, getting into his car. "Sure it will."

Two hours later, right at seven, Jessica pulled up to the Beach Cafe in Lila's lime-green Triumph. Her heart was pounding, and her hands trembled as she pulled the key from the ignition. Any second now she would see him, hold him, kiss him.

Slamming the car door shut behind her, she ran eagerly up the boardwalk steps to the cafe. Her heart thudded in her throat as she saw the lone figure standing at the edge of the patio that overlooked the ocean. For a moment she just stood there and stared.

His thick, tawny-blond hair curled in the salt air. His shoulders were broad beneath his pine-green polo shirt. His powerful chest tapered to a flat waist and narrow hips encased in soft, worn blue jeans.

Jessica nervously smoothed her black tank dress down with her hands and hoped that her hair hadn't gotten too wind tossed in Lila's car.

Then, as though he had felt the tug of her eyes, he turned to look at her. His expression was unreadable, and Jessica felt a moment of panic. She was uncharacteristically unsure of herself with him—he was so much older, more experienced, more sophisticated than any boy she had known. That's what the difference was, she realized. She had known only boys; he was a man.

She forced her feet to move forward as he began to close the distance between them. Suddenly they were face-to-face, and his dark eyes bored into hers, searching their blue depths as if to decipher her feelings. Unable to speak, Jessica stared at him, longing to touch him, to have him hold her, to tell her everything would be all right.

When he finally reached for her and pulled her against his warm chest, she breathed a shaking sigh of relief. Leaning against him, she curled her arms around his neck and inhaled his clean, soapy scent. This was heaven. She knew she didn't deserve it, but she had it.

"Jess, I was afraid you wouldn't come," he said into her hair.

"Of course I came," she said softly. "I want to be with you—you know that."

"How have you been?" he asked, releasing her and leading her over to where his car was parked.

"Not great," she admitted, brushing her blond bangs off her face. "You know Sue is staying at my parents' house for a while, right?" She climbed into the car and settled back against the seat.

Jeremy nodded, starting the engine.

"So it looks like I'll be at Lila's for a while. My folks are so mad right now, it's probably a good idea."

Jeremy reached over and laced his fingers through hers. "I'm sorry you have to go through this," he said.

Jessica smiled at him. "It's worth it."

Jeremy kissed her hand, keeping his eyes on the road. "I thought we could go to a little Mexican place up the coast a bit. I figured we wouldn't want to run into anyone we knew."

Jessica nodded, relishing Jeremy's presence, the sight of him, the sound of his voice.

Forty minutes later they were seated at a window table in a small restaurant right on the ocean. The mood was romantic, with soft candlelight washing their faces, and the faint strains of Spanish guitars floating in the night air.

After they had ordered, Jeremy said, "Jessica, I want to do what's best for you—"

"What's best for me is to be with you," she said urgently, leaning closer to him across the table.

"Jessica—you're only sixteen." He seemed pained to have to remind them both of the hard facts. "You still have college ahead of you—"

He grimaced and looked out over the water, and

when she took his hand in hers, he gripped back so strongly she almost cried out.

"Look, Jeremy, we'll work it out somehow," Jessica said. "The important thing is for us to be together. That's all that matters. We love each other. That's all we need to know. And now that the wedding is out of the way, we can start dealing with the details." She smiled at him, willing him to see the truth that was plainly in front of them.

Jeremy raised tortured eyes to her face. Taking both her hands in his, he reached down to press a kiss into her open palm, and Jessica felt shivers run down her spine.

"Do you really feel that way?" Jeremy asked.

"You know I do."

Jessica almost jumped when their waiter suddenly appeared with their order. Her hand dropped away from Jeremy's, and they both waited tensely while the waiter bustled about, moving their candle and setting down plates of steaming, delicious-smelling food. Finally he was gone.

Silently Jeremy took a sip of the beer he had ordered. Jessica watched the amber liquid in the tilted glass. Dating someone old enough to drink seemed risky and exciting.

Suddenly sitting back in his chair, Jeremy seemed to have reached a decision. "I was hoping that you would say that, Jessica. I know we have a long, hard road ahead of us, but I wanted to give you this, as a symbol of my commitment to you. For today, tomorrow, and forever."

While Jessica watched incredulously, Jeremy

pulled out a small midnight-blue velvet box from his pocket. He set it on the table between them and opened the lid.

Jessica stared, feeling faint. Her face flushed, then paled, and when she looked up at Jeremy, her pupils were almost black.

"Wha—wha?" was all she could manage.

Inside the velvet box was a ring. It was a gold band with a large blue sapphire as dark as the sky at night. A sparkling diamond glittered brightly on each side of it. It was the ring that Jessica had shown Jeremy almost a month ago at Bibi's, the ring she had said was her favorite. Her engagement ring.

Slowly Jeremy took the ring from the box and slid it onto the third finger of her left hand, which was suddenly ice-cold. Then he clasped her hands in his and said very solemnly, "Jessica, will you marry me? Will you be my wife?"

For long moments Jessica could only stare at Jeremy, then at the ring shining on her finger, then back at Jeremy. Finally a smile like sunlight broke across her face, and she said in a low voice, "Yes, of course, Jeremy. Of course I'll marry you." Jessica *Randall*.

Across the table the love of her life beamed at her. He bent down and kissed her hands. "You've made me very happy, Jessica. I know it will be a long time until we can marry, but I promise that I'm yours until then."

Jessica lovingly stroked his cheek. "It will only be two years, Jeremy. As soon as I'm eighteen, we can elope, if my parents are still against our being together."

Raising his glass of beer in a toast, Jeremy said, "To us. And may the next two years pass quickly."

"To us," Jessica agreed, raising her glass of iced tea.

The rest of the meal seemed to float by in a dream. Jessica wasn't even aware of what she was eating. All she was conscious of was Jeremy's smile, his voice, his dark, compelling eyes across the table. She ate methodically, thinking ahead to when they could be alone again, and she would be in his arms.

The sparkling ring on her finger caught her eye time after time. It was the most beautiful ring she had ever seen. The idea that she would be wearing it now, and that Jeremy would be her fiancé, seemed almost unbelievable. She was sure that no girl had ever been as happy as she was at that very moment. *Except Sue.* Shaking her head, Jessica quickly banished the thought.

After dinner Jeremy ordered coffee for them both. It was hot and strong, and floating with cream.

Reaching across the table for her hand, Jeremy smiled at her. "Are you happy?" he asked.

"You know I am." Jessica's eyes shone at him.

For a moment Jeremy looked away, out at the water. "If I have to have you back at Lila's by ten, we'd better get going. But there's something I have to tell you first."

Jessica leaned forward. "Jeremy, what is it?" A tiny flicker of fear gripped her heart. He suddenly looked so serious.

"It's about us. You know my job is in New York, right? Well—I talked to them last night, to tell them I would be back sooner than I expected, since I wasn't going on a—honeymoon. And they offered me a field assignment down in Costa Rica."

"Costa Rica?"

"Jessica, I took it. I leave on Friday. I'll be gone about three or four weeks."

"What? Jeremy, you can't be serious. Now that we can finally be together, how can you take off like this?"

"Jessica, please try to understand. I'm doing this for you as much as for me. We need to give everyone a chance to cool down. We need to give this town a chance to let the whole thing blow over. And we need to give Sue a chance to get herself together and go back to her job in New York. I mean, what if the stress causes her to have some kind of relapse with her blood disease?"

Suddenly a clear image shot through Jessica's brain. Back in New York, Jeremy and Sue would still work side by side at Project Nature. Sue would look pale and needy. Jeremy would feel guilty and obligated. And Jessica would be here in Sweet Valley. Had she won Jeremy only to lose him again down the line?

As though he had read her mind, Jeremy said, "Another reason I took this assignment is that it will help me get transferred to the Los Angeles office of Project Nature. I've applied for a transfer. Once Sue is back on her feet, she'll be able to handle New York on her own."

Jessica relaxed in her seat. "I'm sure she will. Having you here permanently would be wonderful, Jeremy. But I'm going to miss you so much while you're gone. Costa Rica is so far away. You're leaving on Friday?"

Nodding, Jeremy said, "Yeah. But I'll be back before you know it. And then everything will be different, you'll see." A private smile played around the corners of his mouth.

"OK," Jessica said bravely. "If you think it's best. At least we can spend the rest of the week together. And I'll drive you to the airport on Friday," she said decisively. "It's the least I can do."

Jeremy sat back in surprise. "Oh, honey, you don't have to do that. I can take a cab."

"No, of course I want to." Jessica smiled at him lovingly. "It'll give us a few extra moments together."

"Well, OK," Jeremy agreed reluctantly. "There's something else I want to talk to you about. I'd like you to keep our engagement a secret until I get back from my assignment. Will you do that for me?"

"But, Jeremy, why?" Jessica was so proud of her ring—she was dying to show it off. In her mind she had already anticipated the shocked and envious reactions of her friends.

"For all the same reasons that I'm going away. We need to give everything a chance to blow over. Let everyone cool down, let Sue go back to New York, let your parents quit hassling you. You understand, don't you? After I come back, we can make the announcement and officially be a couple. OK? Will you do that for me?"

Gazing into Jeremy's loving, fathomless eyes, Jessica felt there was nothing she could refuse him. And what he said did make sense. "Yes, Jeremy," she found herself agreeing. "We'll keep our engagement a secret until you get back."

Much later that night Jessica lay in bed at Lila's house, dreamily watching the patterns of shadows dance across the moonlit walls of her room. *Mrs. Jeremy Randall. Jessica Wakefield-Randall. Mr. and Mrs. Wakefield-Randall.* Smiling with a deep inner satisfaction, Jessica rolled onto her side and drew her left hand out from beneath the pillow. Her sapphire glinted darkly, as though it were a bottomless pool of water. The diamonds caught a stray moonbeam and splashed a crazy sunburst pattern over her walls.

It was going to absolutely kill her to keep this to herself until Jeremy returned. But she had promised him. And for the first time in her life, it seemed very important that she keep a promise.

Chapter 4

"Good morning, Sue," Elizabeth said as she entered the kitchen on Friday morning. It was another typically glorious southern-California late-summer morning, clear and sunny and sure to be very hot later. "Did you sleep well?" For Elizabeth the week had seemed to drag slowly by. Each day there were little household chores, errands, details to take care of, and each hour of the day was colored by worrying about Sue. And about Jessica and Jeremy. Ever since Sue had told her about her mother's distrust of Jeremy, Elizabeth had been wondering more and more what lay in store for Jessica.

"Uh-huh," Sue replied listlessly. "But those stupid pills make me feel so groggy in the morning." Slowly she turned the page of the newspaper.

Elizabeth frowned to herself as she got the juice out of the fridge. Earlier in the week Mrs. Wakefield had taken Sue to a psychiatrist, who had prescribed a mild tranquilizer and also sleeping pills to help her get through this difficult time. While Elizabeth had to admit that the drugs had seemed to help Sue break the cycle of endless crying jags and sleepless, frantic nights, she wasn't so sure that relying on prescriptions was the way to get over heartbreak.

"How about some waffles?" she offered brightly, pulling a bag of frozen ones out of the freezer. "I can pop some in the toaster for you."

"No, thanks. I'm not really hungry." Sue took a sip of coffee.

Elizabeth sighed. "How about if I make little airplane noises for you?" she suggested, miming holding up a fork for Sue. She was rewarded by a glimmer of a smile.

"Thanks anyway."

After fixing her waffles and her own cup of coffee, Elizabeth came to sit at the kitchen table. "Listen, Sue, I don't have any plans today, and I was wondering if you wanted to go to the mall with me. We could stop in at the Silver Door salon and get the works—a facial, manicure, a haircut . . . what do you say? My treat. Then we could go splurge on new outfits, something autumnish."

For a moment Sue looked wistful. Then, sighing, she shook her head. "I don't think so, Elizabeth. But I appreciate the offer. Maybe later I'll take a bike ride, or a drive."

Elizabeth forced herself to eat her waffles calmly, thinking about her next plan of attack. She had to do something. Sue was practically wasting away right in front of her. Her hair was lank, she looked pale and wan, and Elizabeth thought she had even lost a few pounds. Several times in the past week Sue had gone off by herself for long walks or bike rides, and each time Elizabeth had worried until Sue came back. *She shouldn't be exerting herself like this,* Elizabeth fretted. *She looks awful. Has her blood disease flared out of remission? Is Sue becoming deathly ill, minute by minute?* It was all Elizabeth could do to hide the cold, sinking feeling in the pit of her stomach. Elizabeth thought back to that day only a couple of weeks ago, when Sue had told her that tests showed she'd developed the same rare blood disease that had killed her mother. *Not even that was enough to make Jeremy stay,* Elizabeth thought bitterly. How could Jessica accept what Jeremy had done to Sue? How could she want a man so willing to be disloyal?

Just then Mrs. Wakefield came into the kitchen. "Morning, girls," she said, heading for the coffee-maker. "Whew, I'm glad it's Friday. It's been a long week." After adding sugar to her mug, she joined the girls at the table. "Any plans for today?"

They both shook their heads. Elizabeth sent a warning glance to her mother, as if to say, *Just look at Sue. There's something very wrong.*

But Mrs. Wakefield sat quietly reading the paper and sipping her coffee. Elizabeth glanced at her now and then, thinking that her mother seemed uncharacteristically tense and brittle. So did her father. Elizabeth knew that they were both worried about Jessica, and about Sue as well. The situation was taking a toll on all of them.

When Mrs. Wakefield had finished her coffee,

she picked up her leather briefcase and said, "Well, I'm off to work now. I thought I'd try to get home early today. Maybe the three of us could go to the beach this afternoon."

Elizabeth smiled. "That would be great, Mom. Like old times." *Except that Jessica won't be there, and wouldn't be welcome if she was.*

The electronic jangle of the doorbell startled all of them before Sue could reply. With a quick glance at the clock, Mrs. Wakefield went to answer it. "Who in the world could it be at this hour?" she wondered aloud.

"So doesn't going to the beach later sound fun?" Elizabeth asked Sue after Mrs. Wakefield had left the kitchen.

"Hmm," Sue replied noncommittally.

Elizabeth almost screamed with frustration. If Sue didn't start making some progress soon, she was going to shake her.

"Sue, could I speak to you alone, please?" A few minutes later Mrs. Wakefield had returned to the kitchen, looking shocked.

"Mom, what is it?" Elizabeth had never seen her mother look that way before.

But Mrs. Wakefield just shook her head and motioned Sue toward the living room. Then Elizabeth noticed that her mother was holding a certified-mail envelope. Sue, looking mystified, followed Mrs. Wakefield out of the kitchen.

Elizabeth sat at her place, chewing her lip. What could it be? Had her mother gotten some bad news in the mail? What kind of information came in a registered letter?

Her coffee mug was halfway to her mouth when Elizabeth's eyes suddenly widened. *Medical-test results, for one thing.* Had Sue just gotten news about more blood tests? Her wan appearance and lack of energy might be caused by something more than the wedding disaster—maybe her horrible blood disease was already starting to manifest itself. Maybe Sue was dying.

Gulping, Elizabeth knotted her fingers and sat staring at the kitchen table. A lump came to her throat as she thought about what a short, unhappy life Sue had led so far. She had lost her mother and her fiancé in such a sort time. Now her very life looked as though it were going to be snuffed out—sooner than anyone could have expected.

Elizabeth quickly reached a decision. The burden of helping Sue through this difficult time had fallen largely on her shoulders: Jessica was gone and was the cause of Sue's unhappiness, anyway; Jeremy was gone, and Mr. and Mrs. Wakefield were at work much of the time. Now Sue was about to receive a blow that would destroy her peace of mind even further. Elizabeth had to know what it was.

Seconds later Elizabeth had slipped noiselessly down the hall and was crouched in front of the closed living-room door, her eye to the keyhole. She had never in her life eavesdropped the way she was doing now, but if anyone had a right to, she did. After all, what concerned Sue concerned her. The knowledge would only help her continue to help Sue.

Sue and Alice Wakefield were sitting side by side on the couch. Mrs. Wakefield was holding up the registered letter. Elizabeth strained to hear her mother's voice.

". . . and the terms of your mother's will were quite explicit, dear," Elizabeth heard Mrs. Wakefield say gently. "If you proceeded with your plans to marry Jeremy, you would be disinherited, and your mother's considerable fortune would be left to others."

Elizabeth's eyes widened. Ever since Sue had told her that she had forfeited her MealQuick inheritance for love, Elizabeth had looked at her in a whole new light. Now part of the mystery was being cleared up.

"I know, Aunt Alice," Sue said evenly. "I guess it'll probably go to my stepfather, Phil Schmitt, now. But it's OK. I'll be able to support myself on what I make at Project Nature, and the money didn't mean that much to me anyway." Suddenly Elizabeth heard Sue's voice break, and, peering through the keyhole, she could see Sue's slim figure crumple onto the couch. "I would give up all the money again, if I could just have Mom back," she said softly through her tears.

Mrs. Wakefield stroked Sue's brown hair off her face. "Actually, dear, the money wasn't left to Mr. Schmitt. The letter I received this morning was from your mother's lawyers. And Nancy apparently made some interesting provisions in her will. In the event of your marriage to Jeremy, the money would actually have been left to me, to use or dispense with as I see fit."

"To you?" Elizabeth saw Sue sit up and wipe her

eyes, then seem to look over at the door Elizabeth was crouched behind. "Did you hear something? No, Mom didn't tell me that the money would go to you." Sue reached forward and took Mrs. Wakefield's hands. "But I'm glad, Aunt Alice. I know that Mom did everything for the best, and I'm happy that you'll get the money."

Elizabeth, her hand clamped over her mouth to prevent another surprised squeak like the one that had almost given her away, could see Sue smiling bravely at Alice Wakefield.

"But that's just it, Sue. The money came to me only if you married Jeremy. But because the marriage was—called off, your inheritance reverts back to you. You'll receive your mother's money after all." She leaned forward to hug Sue, and they disappeared from Elizabeth's sight for a moment.

"You're kidding. Because Jeremy dumped me, I saved my inheritance?" Sue seemed bemused.

"Well, yes, sort of," Mrs. Wakefield replied, looking at the letter she still held. "The terms of your mother's will state that if you end your association with Jeremy Randall, forgoing your engagement, and stay separated from him for the period of not less than two months, then you get your rightful legacy."

Sue nodded and sighed. "Obviously I'm not going to see Jeremy for two months. But all the money in the world won't buy me true love, Aunt Alice," she said sadly.

Outside in the hall Elizabeth rocked back on her heels. So Sue was going to get her money after all. A troubling thought creased Elizabeth's brow. What had Jeremy really thought of Sue's losing her inheritance? Deep inside, Elizabeth couldn't help wondering if Jeremy had left Sue because she had been written out of her mother's will. If he had, what would he do now that she had the money back? And where would that leave Jessica?

But Jeremy aside, maybe this was the turning point Sue needed, Elizabeth thought. Maybe having a fortune to handle would help snap Sue back into the real world. After all, she could do a lot of good with her money—give to charity, set up trust funds and scholarships . . . Elizabeth resolved to help Sue find the best and most fulfilling use for her inheritance. And if Sue wanted to go to Rodeo Drive in L.A. and blow it all on mink-lined bathrobes, well, Elizabeth would help her do that, too. What were friends for?

"Don't worry about a thing—I'll return your rental car for you," Jessica said, trying to appear brave and mature on the outside. On the inside she was screaming, *Don't leave me!* but she didn't want Jeremy to know that. For the first time in her life she was competing not only against girls her own age, whom she never really considered actual competition, but against women older than she was as well. She considered it a miracle that a twenty-three-year-old man like Jeremy had fallen for her, and for the first time in her life she felt insecure about her appeal. Above all else, she wanted to seem grown up, sophisticated, not needy. She wanted to appear more worldly, more accepting, less clingy than Sue had.

Maybe then she would be able to keep him, the man she loved. Because losing him would be worse than death.

Walking through the airport, holding hands, Jessica tried not to show how devastated she felt at the thought of Jeremy's being gone for almost a month. What if he met someone else? What if he forgot about her? Suddenly she had a terrible premonition that this was the last time she and Jeremy would ever be truly happy with each other, as though everything they had said, everything that had happened, even their engagement, was just an illusion.

She tried to shake off the feeling. Walking through the airport, she kept her shoulders back and her head high, not only to look calm and confident, but also because if she slouched, she would ruin the lines of her new blue knit halter dress.

"You look good enough to eat," Jeremy murmured as they walked toward his gate.

Jessica turned to smile at him. "I wanted to make sure you remembered what I look like," she said softly. "Now, you have your ticket, right? And your boarding pass?"

Jeremy nodded. "Took care of all that yesterday. This week has flown by, Jess. But I'm glad we got to spend so much time together."

Jessica brushed a piece of imaginary lint off his sleeve. "I'm glad too. I know I'm going to miss you, but at least I can think about all the good times we've had this week."

At gate 11B Jeremy paused to read what time the flight was expected to take off. "Looks like I have a

51

little while," he said. "Sit down with me a minute so we can talk."

They found two orange plastic seats next to each other, and Jessica set down the round canvas tote she had been carrying for him. He dropped his large backpack onto the floor.

"Oh, I almost forgot," Jessica said, taking her address book out of her purse. "Let me have your mailing address down in Costa Rica, so I can write to you." She smiled up at him, her blue-green eyes made even deeper by the blue of her dress. Crossing one slim, tan leg over the other, she pretended not to notice his admiring gaze as she pulled the cap off her pen.

Jeremy looked down at her, an amused smile on his handsome face. "Address?"

Giggling, Jessica said, "Of course, silly. I have to be able to send you love letters." She dropped her voice. "I want to write to you every day, so you know I love you and I'm always thinking of you."

Jeremy clasped her hand between his, seeming at a loss for words. "Gosh, you know, Jess, I don't think I have the complete address written down."

Confusion spread across Jessica's heart-shaped face. "You don't know where you're going?"

"No, I do know," he corrected her. "But at the airport down there a car will come pick me up. I made all the arrangements through the office in New York, so I don't have the exact zip code or even the area code for the phone." He shrugged, a regretful smile on his face. "But I tell you what. As soon as I land in Costa Rica, I'll call you and give you the address and a phone number where you can call me. OK?"

Jessica's face relaxed. "Yeah. You have Lila's number, right?"

Jeremy nodded, brushing his hand across Jessica's bare back. Her skin tingled where his fingers touched. "I'm really going to miss you, Jess," he said huskily. "I'll be counting the minutes until we're together again."

Hardly trusting herself to speak, Jessica nodded. "Me, too," she whispered.

"Do you think you'll still be at Lila's when I come back?"

"I don't know. Probably I'll be home before then. When Sue goes back to New York. I hope she goes soon." Jessica made a grimace.

"Have you talked to her recently?" Jeremy asked, running his fingers through her long blond hair.

"Me? No. I haven't seen her since the wedding. Once I called Elizabeth at home, but when Sue answered, I just hung up." Jessica shrugged. "I just didn't feel like dealing with her. I mean, I don't hate the girl or anything, but I don't want to go on a big guilt trip just because I won and she lost." She looked down at her lap and played with the hem of her skirt.

Jeremy laughed softly, then brushed his lips against her cheek. "That's OK, sweetie," he said. "There's no reason you should talk to her. In fact, for her sake it'd probably be better if you didn't."

A glaring voice over the loudspeaker announced that Jeremy's flight was about to board. Jessica suddenly felt as though her heart were on fire. How would she live without Jeremy for the next month?

What would she do with herself? Every minute of every hour of every day her mind would be on him, missing him, wishing he were with her, wishing he were holding her. Would he be feeling the same? Would he still love her?

"OK, sweetie, I have to go," Jeremy said gently. He stood up.

"I'll stay till your plane takes off," Jessica said, trying not to let her voice waver.

"No, no, don't be silly. I want you to leave right now—just turn around and walk away. I want to remember how beautiful you look right this minute. And the whole time I'm gone, I'll be thinking of how brave you were when we said good-bye. OK?"

"I want to stay," Jessica said stubbornly, her hands nervously playing with a button on the front of his shirt. She couldn't bear to look up into his coffee-dark eyes.

Jeremy took her hands in his and said firmly, "Listen, Jessica. This won't be easy on either of us, but you have to be strong. I want you to kiss me good-bye, turn, and walk out of here before I board. Walk away and don't look back, then before you know it, I'll come home and we can be together. Promise me."

Jessica didn't say anything.

The loudspeaker announced the second level of boarding.

"Jessica, I'll call you as soon as I get there and give you the address. Now kiss me good-bye and go home." He spoke firmly but not unkindly.

Obediently Jessica turned her face upward to his and was rewarded by his lips coming down to meet

54

hers. For long moments they kissed; then gently Jeremy disengaged himself.

"I love you, Jessica," he whispered. "I'll see you in no time. Then we can announce our engagement. Have you told anyone about it?"

Jessica shook her head, her eyes swimming in unshed tears. "No," she choked out.

"Good girl." Jeremy bent his head swiftly and captured her lips again, then again pushed her away and aimed her at the exit.

Swallowing a sob, Jessica dashed her tears away with the back of her hand, then started walking backward toward the exit. "'Bye, Jeremy," she whispered. "See you soon."

"'Bye, sweetheart. Don't forget I love you."

Jessica swallowed hard again, then nodded.

Jeremy made shooing motions with his hands, a loving smile on his face.

Then, mustering all the will she could, Jessica turned and walked away. She swallowed quickly several times and wiped away her tears once more. Just once she turned back and saw Jeremy still watching her, still smiling after her, still blowing her kisses. Then she left and didn't look around again. It wasn't until she was sitting in Jeremy's rental car in the airport parking lot that she finally let go, let the sobs burst out of her and the tears roll down her face.

When the doorbell rang later on Friday evening, Elizabeth flew out of her room and headed downstairs. "I'll get it!" she yelled. Since the wedding fiasco on Saturday, she hadn't been able to get together with Todd, her boyfriend. Between his part-time job and Elizabeth's staying home to keep Sue company, days had gone by when they only talked on the phone. But Sue had urged her to go out.

"I'll be fine," she said. "I have a new magazine to read, and I rented a movie. You go have a good time with Todd."

So Elizabeth had taken her at her word. Now she was almost breathless with excitement, as though it were their first date. She had really missed him this week. Tonight she had taken extra care with her appearance and was wearing a short white denim skirt with a sleeveless plaid cotton blouse knotted at her waist.

Smiling with anticipation, she flung open the front door. But her greeting died on her lips when she saw Todd standing there, smiling at her.

"Well?" he asked with an eager grin. "What do you think?" He struck a mock model's pose in the doorway, his hands curled into fists and his body turned sideways.

"You have a new haircut," Elizabeth said mechanically.

"Yep!" he said proudly. "Notice anything else?"

"Uh, you forgot to shave." *Wow, Todd must have rushed over here without looking in the mirror.* It was kind of sweet, how eager he must have been to be on time.

Todd smiled teasingly. "No, I didn't. I'm growing a mustache!"

For a moment Elizabeth was frozen into silence. Surely he must be kidding. That tan fuzz on his upper lip couldn't be there on *purpose*.

56

"A mustache?" she managed.

"Yeah! Cool, huh? After I got this haircut, I started thinking: It's time for a change. I'm older now, taller. I've got more muscle. Let's face it, Elizabeth. I'm not a little kid anymore. So I decided to go with a whole new look. The haircut was just the start. Then I noticed that all the hottest stars have mustaches nowadays. Some of them even have goatees. So why not me?" He beamed at her, stroking his lip fuzz lovingly.

Elizabeth looked at him. "Why not you?" she repeated slowly. *Well, because it just doesn't really suit you?* "Um, well, gosh, Todd. Wow. It certainly is different." She forced a smile. "Let me just grab my purse and we can go."

Half an hour later they were sitting at an outdoor table at Alfalfa's, a new health-food restaurant that Elizabeth had wanted to try.

"It's good to see you, Todd. I've been so upset lately—there just seems to be so much going on."

"Poor baby," Todd said sympathetically. "You told me about Jessica and the whole boarding-school thing. What's the news on that?"

"Mom and Dad are considering setting up an appointment with the headmaster in a couple weeks. I just can't believe it. This whole thing is tearing our family apart. Not only that, but the more I find out about Jeremy and Sue's past relationship, the more I distrust him." Elizabeth had told Todd about Sue's inheritance, and Nancy Gibbons's suspicion about Jeremy. "I can't help worrying about what his motives are with Jessica. She's not rich."

Todd frowned. "Maybe he really loves Jessica. After all, she's beautiful, and she can be a lot of fun when she's not totally out of control." He picked up his menu and began reading.

"I just can't believe he's sincere," Elizabeth insisted. "I don't trust him. At least he'll be gone for a few weeks. Maybe Jessica will realize that she's better off without him."

Todd made a doubtful face. "Yeah. Don't bet on it." He leaned over to take her hand in his and quickly brushed his lips against her cheek. Her skin crawled at the touch of the short bristly hairs above his lip. "I'm sorry you're so upset about it, sweetie. But you know Jessica—she's always in the middle of some flammable situation or another. But she always lands on her feet."

Elizabeth couldn't shake her fear. "This time she's playing in the big leagues, though."

"Liz, just try to put it out of your mind for tonight," Todd pleaded. "I haven't seen you in so long. Let's just enjoy being together tonight, OK?"

Sitting back, Elizabeth managed a smile. She tried to relax. Unfortunately, when she looked at Todd, all she could see was his mustache. And each time she was jolted by the sight. Then a feeling of tenderness came over her. She would let him be silly about his mustache for a few days—after all, how long could it last? As soon as the guys at school saw it, they would get on his case, and he'd get rid of it. She didn't have to worry about it.

"Elizabeth," Todd said softly, gazing deeply into her eyes, "can I ask you something?"

"Yes, Todd?"

"What the heck is textured vegetable protein?" he asked, pulling back and pointing at the menu. "It sounds disgusting."

Elizabeth read the menu. "I think it's like tofu, sort of. Sort of like dried tofu that they crumble up and form into patties or loaves or whatever. It's supposed to be a good substitute for meat."

"Yum," Todd said uncertainly. "Dried, crumbled tofu. Maybe I'll just have the stir-fry." He tossed his menu aside and leaned forward again. "You look great tonight."

"Thank you." Elizabeth took a sip of her water, then smiled across the table at Todd. She reached out and took his hand. He grinned at her. She had always loved his grin. Of course, now she could barely see it.

"I felt kind of weird, leaving Sue at home like this. I mean, my parents are there, but she should be with people her own age."

Todd sighed almost imperceptibly. "It must be awful to be left at the altar like that in front of everybody," he said, appearing to accept the fact that Elizabeth was too wrapped up in what was happening at home to let it go. "On the other hand, if Jeremy really loves Jessica more than Sue, it would be wrong for him to marry Sue." He shook his head, puzzling over the convoluted situation.

The waitress came to take their order then, and Elizabeth ordered a vegetarian burrito. They both asked for iced teas.

"So you sympathize with Jeremy?" Elizabeth asked when they were alone again.

"Not really sympathize," Todd clarified. "I think it's awful what he did, running out on the wedding like that. But I don't think we should sentence him to a lifetime of unhappiness just because he made a mistake, either." He knit his brows in confusion. "Like, what if I had dated someone else my whole life and had never met you. Say I liked this girl a whole lot, and we seemed like a good couple. So we get engaged, and everybody's happy. Then, right before the wedding, I meet you. I would fall in love with you and know that you're who I really should be with. I would have to get out of the engagement somehow. I probably wouldn't do it in the middle of the wedding, though," he finished.

Elizabeth nodded slowly, picking at the nonfat chips and salsa on their table. When Todd explained it that way, it made a little more sense. But somehow she couldn't help feeling that the situation with Sue, Jeremy, and Jessica was more complicated than that. For one thing, Todd's mythical other girlfriend wasn't an heiress.

Chapter 5

Ten days. Ten sad, lonesome, endless days without Jeremy. Silently Jessica regarded her face in the mirror. Did she look older, more mature? She thought so. No doubt getting engaged to be married had given her this new look of serenity, of wisdom. For the last two weeks she had been hugging her secret engagement tightly to herself, letting it comfort her during Jeremy's absence. It was the longest by far she had ever kept anything from anyone, especially Elizabeth or Lila. The weight of it was starting to rankle.

"Jess, have you seen my navy-blue mascara?" Lila asked, coming up behind her. They were getting ready for school.

"Right here." Without turning away from her reflection in the bathroom mirror, Jessica held up the tube.

"I can't believe it's only Wednesday," Lila mumbled, outlining her lips with red pencil. "I'm ready for it to be the weekend."

Jessica smiled. "You're *always* ready for it to be the weekend. How are things with the Rob-man?" Should she tell Lila? Jeremy had asked her not to . . . but he hadn't *forbidden* her to. It felt unnatural, keeping her engagement a secret. Especially when Lila was prattling on about her boring relationship with Robby. Jessica was a *real* woman, an engaged woman. Lila should know.

Expertly Lila filled in her lips with matching lip gloss, then started doing her lashes. "Great, as usual. He's been really busy, preparing several of his paintings for his opening. I told you Daddy agreed to let him use that portrait of me, right? Robby says it'll be the centerpiece of the whole show."

"That's really exciting. When is the show?" Jessica leaned over and fluffed her hair, then stood up quickly and patted it into place. *I think I'll tell her. I have to tell her.*

"Not until practically Christmas. I don't know why they're starting to plan it so early, but there you go." Lila patted her lips with a tissue and regarded herself in the mirror. "Oh! But guess what? I had the most brilliant idea." She turned to look at Jessica excitedly. "I enrolled Robby for a business course at Sweet Valley University!"

Jessica looked at her blankly. "What do you mean?"

"I signed him up for a business course. You know how worried I've been about his business sense. The way these gallery people are taking advantage of him is practically criminal. So I signed him up and paid the fees and everything. He should be getting the notice any day now."

I'd like to be a fly on the wall when Robby finds out about this. Jessica gathered up her books, then waited for Lila to put on her watch and earrings.

"Girls! Let's go," Mrs. Fowler called. Lila grinned at Jessica.

"Coming, Mom!" Lila grabbed her briefcase containing her schoolbooks, and they went out into the hall. "We have to move the Triumph so she can get her car out," Lila explained. "But anyway, as I was saying, Robby should hear about it any day now. I bet he's going to be thrilled. After all, I have only his best interests at heart. And he could never afford the business course himself."

Yeah, yeah. Now, be quiet so I can tell you about the most important thing that's ever happened to me in my whole life.

The girls waved good-bye to Lila's mother, who was looking chic in an off-white business suit, with an Hermès scarf thrown over her shoulder.

Lila started the engine of her lime-green Triumph. Jessica turned to her in the front seat and cleared her throat.

Well, here goes. "I have something to tell you about Jeremy," Jessica said, taking out her sunglasses.

Lila looked at her with frank interest. "Do, do."

"Well, he finally has a mailing address and phone number, so I'm going to mail him all the letters I've been writing—one a day for each of the ten days he's been gone. Maybe I'll even call him." Jessica couldn't keep the pride out of her voice. True, Lila's Robby was adorable and talented and a sexy eighteen-year-old, but no one could hold a candle to Jeremy.

Jessica swallowed, feeling an uncharacteristic sense of guilt. She *had* promised Jeremy that she wouldn't tell anyone, but he hadn't meant her very best friend in the whole world, had he? Of course not. He would understand. And she had to tell someone. If she could talk to Lila about the actual engagement, she might miss Jeremy less, she reasoned. She had already kept it secret for more than two weeks. That was much longer than she had thought she'd be able to.

At the next red light she turned to look at Lila, her face glowing with excitement. "Li, can you keep a secret? I mean, a really big, really important secret?"

Lila lowered her sunglasses to peer at Jessica. "Of course," she said. "You know me."

Phhtt! The spitball shot over the corner of Elizabeth's desk and hit Scott Trost in the arm. He swung around and saw Charlie Cashman triumphantly holding up an empty pen cartridge. Scott grinned, and Elizabeth saw him quickly tear off a corner of his notebook page and start to wad it up. She sighed.

Another day, another trig class. It was always like this. For some reason math seemed to bring out the worst in the male species.

Mr. Harrison, the trig teacher, demonstrated a problem on the board, then asked for solutions.

Here we go. Wearily, Elizabeth raised her hand,

and so did Penny Ayala, Todd, and Dana Larson.

But before Mr. Harrison could call on anyone, Ken Matthews shouted out the answer. With a curt nod the teacher indicated that he had answered correctly and went on to demonstrate another problem.

"All right!" Ken said, and gave his desk a brief drumroll. A couple of his football-team buddies made approving whistling noises and whoops.

Elizabeth rolled her eyes and looked around the class. She caught Todd's eye and made a face. He smiled. Elizabeth looked away. His limp, tan mustache was getting longer all the time, but it didn't seem to be getting thicker. It was sort of long and thin and straight. Like a caterpillar in a rainstorm.

Mr. Harrison called on Molly Adams to answer the next question, and when Charlie Cashman tried to yell it out, she shushed him and waited for Molly to answer. Molly looked up, startled, and blushed faintly. Elizabeth didn't know her that well; this was the first class they had ever had together. Molly seemed very shy and quiet.

Charlie was bouncing in his seat and tapping his feet impatiently, bursting to yell out the answer. Several other people raised their hands.

Then Molly whispered something.

"What was that?" Mr. Harrison asked kindly. "I didn't quite hear you."

"Um, X equals forty-five?" Molly said timidly.

Charlie, Scott, and some of the other boys started to snicker. Molly blushed harder and seemed to sink down farther in her seat.

Mr. Harrison made a regretful face. "I think

you forgot to factor in the cosine equivalent," he said, then turned to solve the problem on the board.

"I know, I know!" Danny Porter yelled.

Mr. Harrison turned around and said, "Very well, Danny, what is it?"

As Danny rattled off the answer, Elizabeth sighed again. She couldn't wait for English class.

"Liz! Wait up!"

Elizabeth turned to see Enid hurrying down the hall toward her.

"Anything good for lunch today?" Enid asked.

Elizabeth looked up to read the menu board over the hot-lunch counter. "Nope. Not unless chicken potpie, vegetable medley, spiced applesauce, and your choice of an apple or orange is your idea of a good lunch."

"Remind me to brown-bag it tomorrow," Enid said dryly, and Elizabeth laughed.

They got in line and took trays off the steaming, still-wet pile at the end of the counter. Soon they were sitting at their usual table in the cafeteria.

"What's wrong? You seem preoccupied," Enid said as she started pushing the chicken potpie around on her plate. "Is it about Sue or Jessica?"

"No, neither, for once. I just had a depressing experience in trig," Elizabeth answered. "Guys are so lame sometimes."

"Whoa! Hey, babe!" Todd swooped down and rubbed his mustache against Elizabeth's cheek. She recoiled, and he laughed.

"Scratchy, huh? Listen, save me a place. Be right back."

Elizabeth watched him head for the lunch line. She and Todd had been together for a long time. She had always been so glad that they were best friends as well as boyfriend and girlfriend. And she had always been so proud of his healthy good looks. When he looked at her with his warm brown eyes, she seemed to melt. It hadn't always been perfect—they had weathered a lot of ups and downs. But somehow they had always managed to see things clearly at the end and stay together. She had always felt really lucky to have him. Until now. Until the mustache.

Throughout the cafeteria several guys from the basketball team stopped Todd to admire his mustache. Ken Matthews slapped him a high five, and Todd stroked the new growth lovingly.

"They seem impressed with Todd's new look," Enid observed, turning her attention back to her lunch.

"Uh-huh." Elizabeth took a bite of vegetable medley.

Shrewdly looking at her best friend, Enid asked, "I take it you're not?"

"You can take it that I'm completely grossed out," Elizabeth whispered. She leaned across the table. "I think it's so repulsive. It's like a fuzzy moth decided to molt on Todd's upper lip. I keep expecting to look and see a cocoon forming."

Enid tried to smother her laughter. "Well, maybe he'll get tired of it soon and shave it off."

"I hope so. I thought that once the guys at school

teased him about it, he would lose it. But they love it! It's so weird. The last few times I've kissed him, I just got totally turned off," Elizabeth whispered. "I mean, I didn't think I was so shallow about looks, and I'm ashamed of myself for letting such a little thing bother me, but I just think it's so icky. Between that and the haircut, I feel like Todd is a complete stranger. He just seems so unattractive to me. He's even acting differently. More testosterony somehow." She pushed her vegetables around on her plate.

Enid nodded sympathetically.

"Yo, Guy!" Todd yelled to Guy Chesney. "Throw me a juice, will you?"

Todd was standing right behind Elizabeth, and he quickly put his tray on the table. Guy threw him a carton of orange juice, which Todd caught expertly. Then he sat down next to Elizabeth.

"Say, Liz, I was wondering if you wanted to come over tonight," Todd said, taking a sip of his juice. "We could go over some of those trig problems. When we do them together, I always seem to understand them better." He smiled at Elizabeth, and she couldn't help smiling back. At least his brown eyes hadn't changed.

"That sounds good," she said. "I'll just check with Sue first to make sure she doesn't need me for anything."

Todd nodded and started to work on the hamburger that he had gotten in the fast-food line.

"How's Sue doing?" Enid asked.

Elizabeth started to peel her orange. "She seems better. Maybe I'm kidding myself, but she does seem a little less despondent lately. She's sleeping better and eating a bit more."

"That's good. Maybe the three of us can take in a movie this weekend." Enid glanced at Todd. "That is, if you're not busy."

"Um-hmm." Elizabeth nodded, eating her orange.

"Elizabeth! It's just the most romantic news! Are you going to be the maid of honor, or what?"

Caroline Pearce leaned over Elizabeth's shoulder, her green eyes gleaming, her nose twitching from the scent of a hot story. Everyone at Sweet Valley High knew she was the biggest gossip in school.

Elizabeth swallowed. "What are you talking about, Caroline?"

Caroline's eyes widened. "I'm talking about Jessica's wedding! After all, she's engaged. So are you going to be her maid of honor? What are you going to wear? Where is it going to be? This is so exciting!"

"Caroline, don't be ridiculous," Elizabeth scoffed. "Jessica isn't engaged. Where did you hear that?"

Caroline drew herself back. "Lila told me," she said pointedly. "And I guess she would know. She said she even saw the ring."

Elizabeth stared at her. Then she stared at Enid, who looked as wide-eyed as she felt.

"Wow," Todd said, eating a french fry.

"Lila must be mistaken somehow," Elizabeth said firmly. "Jessica isn't engaged. She's only sixteen, for godsake!"

"Well, all I know is what Lila told me," Caroline said haughtily. "And she said that Jessica is engaged, and has a ring, and is already thinking about what kind of wedding she wants." With that Caroline turned and flounced away.

After she left, Elizabeth pushed her uneaten food away, then rested her head on her hands. Great. Terrific. Just when Sue was starting to look a teensy bit better, just when Elizabeth had started to hope that everyone would recover from the whole disaster, Jessica had to announce her engagement to Jeremy, slimeball of the Western world. "I'm having a very bad day," she mumbled.

That night after dinner Elizabeth closed the door to her room. For a moment she sat on the bed and looked around. For as long as she could remember, her room had been a haven and a solace. She had chosen the colors herself, and the restful pastel shades never failed to comfort her. Her bed was made, the desk tidy, the closet doors shut. Inside the closet she knew she would find shoes hanging neatly in their shoe bag, clothes lined up according to color and function, and a stack of shoe boxes filled with old letters, photos, ancient diaries . . .

But something was wrong. Elizabeth frowned, taking another look at the room. What was it? Was something out of place? Was something missing? No. That was just it. Everything was exactly as Elizabeth had left it this morning, and the morning before that, and the morning before that. Jessica hadn't come in at any time to borrow something without asking, to take her last stamp, to wear Elizabeth's new sweater before Elizabeth had a chance to wear it herself. It was Jessica. She was missing. She was out of place.

Flopping down onto her bed, Elizabeth thought about Jessica. She really missed her. During Jessica's stay at Lila's, Elizabeth had missed her in a sort of intangible way—missed her presence, missed the excitement that always seemed to buzz around her. But the news this afternoon had brought home a much stronger feeling of lonesomeness and solitude that was depressing and disturbing. Solitude was not a feeling Elizabeth often had. She smiled wryly. No one could feel alone who had Jessica for an identical twin.

Although she knew there was no way, for at least a couple of years, that Jessica could actually get married and leave home for good, still, the knowledge that Jessica wanted to had shaken Elizabeth up. In a sense she felt as if Jessica was willing to leave Elizabeth forever to be with Jeremy. It was one thing to stay at Lila's until a scandal blew over—it was another to commit yourself to a man and be ready to run off with him. Leaving Elizabeth behind. As though they were just regular sisters. Not twins at all. Not only that, but Elizabeth knew her mom and dad were teetering on the brink of sending Jessica away for the next couple of years. The news about Jessica's engagement would probably decide that question once and for all.

Elizabeth rolled over on her bed and took a tissue from the box on her nightstand. For the last two weeks Sue had been her main concern. In her spare time she had felt anger and distrust toward Jeremy, and anger and impatience toward Jessica. Now all she felt was an overwhelming sadness.

71

The first tear had just welled up when the phone rang.

Todd. Oops. We were supposed to study tonight. Elizabeth sniffled and grabbed the phone.

"Hello?"

"Hey," Jessica said breezily.

"Jessica—I was just thinking about you," Elizabeth said.

"I know," Jessica joked. "I picked up on your vibes. Listen, Elizabeth, I don't know if you heard . . ."

"About your engagement? Yeah," Elizabeth said dryly. "Since I happen to attend Sweet Valley High, I couldn't really avoid hearing about it. It's all anyone's talking about."

"Yeah, well." Jessica sounded uncomfortable. "It won't happen for a couple years, anyway."

"Oh, Jess!" Elizabeth suddenly burst out. She forgot about how stupid she thought the engagement was, and how selfish she considered Jessica and Jeremy. She forgot how worried she was about Sue. "I miss you so much! You've been gone for weeks, and I hardly see you at school. And then I find out that you're engaged. . . ." The tears that hadn't come before started to roll down Elizabeth's cheeks, and her voice choked up. "You're getting married and leaving me forever," she sobbed.

"Oh, Lizzie, stop," Jessica said gently. "Don't be silly. It's true that Jeremy and I are engaged, but like I said, that's years away. And even when we do get married, you don't think I could ever leave you behind, do you? Of course not. I'll make Jeremy live wherever you are, no matter what you're doing. And when you get married, you and your husband, Todd, I guess, will live right next door to me and Jeremy. Isn't that what we've always planned?"

Elizabeth sniffled, then blew her nose.

"We're not just family, Liz. We're twins. We're two halves of the same person," Jessica said sincerely. "We always have to be together. I couldn't be happy without you."

"Really?" Elizabeth said.

"Of course. After all, who would take care of me the way you do? Who would be on my side? I mean, I know Jeremy and I are destined to be together and all, but you're actually part of me. I'll only ever have one identical twin." She almost sounded choked up herself.

"That's true," Elizabeth said, sniffling again. "I guess I'm just being silly."

"It's OK," Jessica said. "Just quit worrying. Now, listen, will you be my maid of honor? I promise not to make you wear pink."

Elizabeth groaned. "Please, I don't want to talk about it."

On the other end of the line, Jessica laughed. "OK, OK. Maybe later. What I actually wanted to tell you is that Mom called me a little while ago and asked me to come home again."

"You're kidding. But Sue is still here, and she doesn't have any plans to go back to New York yet."

"I know, but apparently she feels OK about it. At least that's what she told Mom and Dad. So I'm coming home tomorrow after school."

"I'm really glad," Elizabeth said. "But I'm worried

too. I can't believe Sue will be happy about seeing you all the time. Do they know you're engaged?"

"No. I'll wait until it's a good time to tell them."

"Like never."

"No. It'll be soon. I don't care who knows. I did get the impression that the 'rents want to be able to keep a closer eye on me. I guess they think there's not enough supervision at Lila's. Or maybe they just want to spend some time with me before they ship me off to Washington State," she said wryly.

"Oh, Jess, how can you joke about it? Besides, there probably *isn't* enough supervision at Lila's house."

Jessica's tinkling laugh filled Elizabeth's ear. "You say that like it's a bad thing. Anyway, this time tomorrow I'll be rooting through your closet, looking for something new to wear."

"Fine with me," Elizabeth said. *I guess this is what they mean by blood is thicker than water. I know that Jessica's being here is like pouring gasoline on a fire, but I still want her home. I just hope Sue will be able to handle it somehow.*

Chapter 6

When Robby Goodman broke for lunch on Thursday, he decided to save a few bucks by eating leftovers at home instead of grabbing some fast food. He had been earning extra cash that day by scraping and sanding the bottom of Morris Farrell's sailboat, the *Lady Tempest,* at the marina. Morris Farrell was the millionaire industrialist Robby's father worked for, and the Goodmans, father and son, shared a small cottage on the Farrell estate, about five minutes from the marina.

At home Robby absently took in the mail, then headed to the kitchen to make some tuna-fish sandwiches. He was starved. It was a hot day, and he had been working hard all morning. Quickly he ate two sandwiches and considered making a third. He rifled through the mail as he drank a big glass of milk. Mostly stuff for his dad, the new *TV Guide,* an ad for a local video store opening up. Plus there was a large envelope for him from Sweet Valley University. Curious, he opened it.

"Congratulations, Mr. Goodman. We're looking forward to having you in our business class. You'll find your schedule card inside, along with a list of the texts you'll need, which are available at the university bookstore. . . ." Robby read the letter, totally bemused.

This is so weird. There must be some mistake. I'll have to call them. Then his head jerked up, and his blue eyes narrowed in suspicion. *Lila.*

"Enid! Over here!" Elizabeth called, waving her hand. Enid spotted her and smiled, then started working her way through the crowded auditorium to where Elizabeth was sitting. Finally she flopped down in the seat Elizabeth had saved for her.

"Whew. This place is a madhouse. What time is it?" Enid checked her watch. "Great. With any luck this assembly will take us to the end of the day, and we won't have to go back to class. Then there's just one more day, and the week will be over."

Elizabeth nodded, taking out her notebook. "Yeah. Unfortunately, unlike you, who can just space out and grab a little nap during this assembly, I should take notes, in case Mr. Cooper says something I might have to cover for *The Oracle*." Elizabeth was one of the high-school newspaper's top reporters. Working on the paper was giving her invaluable experience in her chosen career: journalism.

Enid smiled knowingly. "You love it. You'd be happy writing an article about a sale on dog food down at the SuperMart."

Elizabeth couldn't help grinning. "You know me too well." She took the cap off her pen with her teeth.

"But this will probably turn out to be announcements for the school-play tryouts or something."

Nodding, Enid said, "Uh-huh. I think I'll just get a head start on my biology homework. Then I can watch TV tonight." She took out her textbook and started highlighting.

Moments later their principal came onstage and tapped the microphone.

"Attention. Attention," Mr. Cooper said, tapping the microphone again. "I've called this assembly in order to announce an exciting new development in our curriculum. Our school has been chosen to participate in an educational experiment that will be taking place all over California."

Elizabeth sat forward. This might actually be interesting.

"They've decided to abolish teachers," Enid whispered, and Elizabeth cracked a smile.

"I don't think that's it," Elizabeth whispered back.

"Statistics show that although male and female students generally perform about the same in math until roughly the second or third grade," Mr. Cooper continued, "after that female students start a steady decline in their math and science abilities."

The principal was interrupted by a guy in the back shouting out, "It's genetic! They're not supposed to be good at math!"

Frowning, Mr. Cooper continued, obviously deciding to ignore the outburst. "Educom, a group of researchers, teachers, and education theorists, have begun instituting a program that has had very interesting results. When they approached me about trying

77

it here at Sweet Valley High, I was most intrigued."

"Cut to the chase," Elizabeth muttered, rapidly writing down what Mr. Cooper was saying.

"Our new program, experimental in nature, is called Girls Only Math, or 'Go Math,'" Mr. Cooper explained. "And it will consist of two math classes in each grade with only female students. After this assembly my assistant will hand out a list of the students affected, along with instructions on when and where their new math classes will meet. Not all students will be included. There will still be some coed math classes, and of course we will also end up having some male-only groups as well. Now, I'd like to talk for a while about the thinking behind this program. . . ."

Chrome Dome Cooper went on to explain the rationale behind the experiment, and Elizabeth feverishly took notes. This assembly would definitely have to be reported on for the newspaper.

Enid leaned over to whisper, "A girls-only math class! I can't believe it."

Nodding, Elizabeth answered grimly, "It's outrageous. Girls are going to be segregated, put off by themselves in special classes, as though we're backward or less capable than boys." It really burned Elizabeth up. "This Go Math program is the stupidest, most sexist thing I've ever heard of," she whispered furiously, "and I'm going to make sure everyone knows it!"

"I can't believe you did that!" Robby shrieked, staring at Lila in disbelief.

It was Thursday afternoon, and Robby had called

Lila after school. Now they were sharing a large order of fries at the Dairi Burger. Lila flipped her brown hair back and grinned at Robby across the table at Sweet Valley's most popular after-school hangout. She leaned forward and took a sip of her root-beer float.

"Don't thank me," she said modestly. "Just do well in the course, and that will be reward enough."

"*Thank* you!" Robby sputtered. He looked around and noticed that people were staring at them. Lowering his voice, he continued, "Lila, I can't believe you did this. It's—it's—well, it's unbelievable."

Lila preened happily while Robby roughly ran his hands through his black hair, making it stand on end. She thought it was so cute when he did that.

"It's no biggie," she insisted. "I was happy to do it. I just want what's best for you. And for you to take this business course at SVU is what's best for you. Simple." She snapped her fingers in the air.

Across the table Robby took several deep breaths. Finally he said, "Lila, you don't understand. I can't believe you signed me up for that business course, because I have no intention of taking it." He leaned across the table earnestly, looking into her eyes. "I know you thought you were doing something nice for me, but we had already discussed this, and I had told you my decision. I'm sorry, but I'm not going to take that class."

"What?" Lila cried. "Why on earth not? I told you—it's all paid for. There's even a credit at the bookstore for the textbooks. I set it all up. There's no reason for you not to take it. If you're worried about the commute—"

Leaning back in his chair, Robby crossed his arms

stubbornly. "The commute is the least of my worries. The main reason is that I don't want to," he said calmly. "I'm an artist, not a businessman. I don't want to waste my time in some business class when I could be working on my art. I told you all this. I have to say, Lila, that I don't appreciate your trying to make up my mind for me." His lips tightened as he looked at her.

Lila sat in her chair, momentarily speechless. "I know you're an artist, Robby. But nowadays even artists have to know something about business. You signed that stupid gallery contract when they're clearly taking advantage of you—a business course would help you avoid doing that in the future."

Robby sighed impatiently. "I'm not interested, Lila. I told you. You can't run my life for me."

"Oh!" A hot flush rose on Lila's cheeks. "I can't believe you're saying this, Robby," she said angrily, trying to keep her voice down. "I'm just looking out for you—not trying to run your life. You know you should take the course. Quit being so stubborn."

"Quit trying to boss me around," Robby said, his eyes glittering with anger. "My feelings count here too, you know. Just cancel the course and get your money back, and we'll forget about it." He stood up and threw some money on the table for their food and drinks.

Lila blinked rapidly to prevent tears from escaping her eyes. "I can't cancel the course," she said plaintively. "I did the early registration. It's nonrefundable. I can't get my money back."

Robby shrugged. "I'm sorry, but it's your own fault.

You can't do big things like this without asking me."

Lila bit her lip. She was so mad she didn't know what she was going to do. Robby was being so stupid and ungrateful that she could hardly look at him. "Robby, it was very expensive," she said in clipped tones. "Are you saying that my money has just been thrown away?" Her nostrils flared as she stared hard in front of her.

Robby stayed on his feet. "Yeah, that's what I'm saying. I'm not a pet, Lila. You can't just make me do anything you want me to do, no matter how much it costs or how bad you want me to do it. I have a mind of my own. I'm sorry you're going to lose that money, but it's your own fault. Now, are you coming or not? I have to get out of here."

"Go ahead," Lila bit out, not looking at him. "I'll get a ride home with someone else."

Robby frowned and looked at the door, then back at Lila. He made an abrupt gesture and said, "Fine. I'll talk to you later."

"Fine."

Lila didn't watch as Robby stormed out the door of the Dairi Burger. She didn't watch as he pulled out of the parking lot in his dad's car. She didn't watch as he disappeared down the street without her.

"I mean, I just can't believe it," Elizabeth raged that night at dinner. Not even Jessica's being home again for the first time in weeks had distracted her from her outrage over the Go Math program. "It's like they just want to hang a banner in front of the school saying, 'Our girls are slow in math.' It really burns me up." She paused for a moment to take some asparagus, then passed the platter on to Sue.

"It does sound kind of sexist," Sue agreed. "On the other hand, last year when I was a senior, I was in calculus. There were only three other girls besides me in that class. I remember thinking that I never got a chance to say anything, because the boys always yelled out the answers. And my teacher—it was such a drag. It was like he'd forgotten that there were even girls in the class. He never called on us. *That's* sexist." She nodded her head definitively.

Elizabeth nodded thoughtfully, then took a bite of her baked chicken. "That's true," she mused, "but then, it seems like the answer would be sensitivity training about sexism, for the teachers, and cracking down on all the piggy boys who don't know how to behave in a classroom." She stabbed her chicken and cut off another bite.

Next to Elizabeth, Mr. Wakefield grinned. "It sounds like this issue has really struck a nerve with you, Elizabeth. Maybe you should do a series of articles, instead of just one. Just be sure to do your research. I have the feeling this Go Math program might have more complicated reasoning behind it than just a bunch of administrators sitting around thinking of ways to humiliate girls."

"Hhmph," Elizabeth said darkly. She glanced around the table, suddenly realizing that she had been dominating the conversation. But maybe that was a good thing. This was the first time Jessica and Sue had seen each other since Jessica had destroyed Sue's wedding and stolen Sue's fiancé.

Elizabeth had to admire Sue's self-control. She

had actually welcomed Jessica home warmly, and had been friendly and interested in what she'd been doing. For her part, Elizabeth had to acknowledge that Jessica had been on her best behavior. Jeremy's name hadn't come up once, and Jessica seemed glad to be home. And, thank heavens, she wasn't flashing her stupid engagement ring. Elizabeth guessed it was in Jessica's jewelry box.

On the whole, everyone was being cheerful and almost artificially normal. Elizabeth wondered when the explosion would occur.

"So, Liz," Jessica said, putting down her glass of milk. "Old Todd is looking pretty foxy lately."

Elizabeth sighed. "I don't want to talk about it," she said. "I guess I just have to wait it out. I mean, how can I say, 'Todd, excuse me, but the lip fringe is a major mistake. And could you please grow your hair out again?'"

Mrs. Wakefield giggled. "I remember when your father decided to update his look. You kids were still tiny." She giggled again.

"What did he do?" Jessica asked.

Mr. Wakefield bristled at his end of the table and pretended to be busy serving himself some salad.

"Well, he grew a mustache, like Todd," Mrs. Wakefield said, grinning at her husband. "However, I must admit, he was older than Todd, and his beard was much fuller and darker. It didn't look too bad."

"Darn right," Mr. Wakefield said huffily.

"But it was the soul patch that got to me," Alice Wakefield continued.

Sue looked puzzled. "What's a soul patch?"

"It's that little place right under the bottom lip, but above the chin." Mrs. Wakefield demonstrated. "Ned had a mustache and just that little patch of beard there. His soul patch."

"Oh, Dad." Jessica looked at her father reproachfully.

"How bad was it?" Elizabeth asked her mother gently.

Mrs. Wakefield tried to smother a laugh. "It could have been worse, I guess. I mean, I didn't actually want to divorce him or anything."

"Darn right," Mr. Wakefield said. "I thought it looked pretty neat." He studiously ate some asparagus.

"Oh. Yes. Neat." Elizabeth nodded knowingly, not trusting herself to look at Jessica.

"Umm, I'm sure it was, Dad. I'm sure it was incredibly—neat," Jessica said carefully, concentrating on her plate.

Then suddenly everyone except Mr. Wakefield dissolved into laughter. They laughed until it hurt, and when Ned looked up, fuming, they laughed even more.

"This is what I get for being in a house of females," Mr. Wakefield said with mock bitterness. But then he looked around the table and smiled tolerantly.

"Oh," said Sue, still laughing. "I remember when Jeremy once—" Abruptly she stopped, the laughter wiped off her face like chalk off a blackboard.

There was a sudden, uncomfortable silence.

"Never mind," Sue said softly, reaching for the water pitcher.

Elizabeth could sense her parents exchanging glances. Then Mr. Wakefield cleared his throat.

"Well, we might as well address the issue, since we're all here," he said calmly. "Sue, you know that we asked Jessica to come home again because we feel that her place is with her family, no matter what the circumstances."

Sue nodded quickly. "Of course it is," she agreed. "There was no reason for Jessica to stay away so long." She took a deep breath. "I won't pretend it hasn't been a difficult situation, but I really don't blame Jessica. Or Jeremy." She looked down at her plate. "It was just one of those things. No one could help it." By the time she finished speaking, her voice was practically a whisper.

Elizabeth ate mechanically, though the food was now tasteless in her mouth. She caught a glimpse of her father's mouth tightening.

"That's very generous of you, Sue," Mrs. Wakefield said warmly. "But we may as well get everything out in the open. Jessica, are you still pursuing a relationship with Jeremy?"

Jessica calmly broke off a piece of her roll and buttered it. "Yes. And he's pursuing one with me."

Elizabeth noticed that she said it firmly, but not brashly—as though she was actually aware of other people's feelings about the matter and trying to be somewhat careful. *This is a first.*

"Where do you think that relationship will lead?" Mr. Wakefield said. "He's seven years older than you. You're still in high school."

"Honey." Mrs. Wakefield put her hand over her

husband's arm, obviously an attempt to make him keep his temper under control.

I should have eaten out tonight, Elizabeth thought, suddenly glum. Then she remembered that Enid had been busy, so she would have had to eat with Todd. In public. With his mustache. She sighed and stirred the salad dressing remaining at the bottom of her bowl.

"Jessica," Mrs. Wakefield said placatingly, "all we're saying is that you're our daughter. We're concerned. We love you and want you to be happy. We just don't want to see you get hurt."

Elizabeth sat in her chair, watching the proceedings out of the corner of her eye. Jessica was remaining remarkably calm. Maybe her love for Jeremy had changed her somehow, matured her. Sue, though she looked a little embarrassed, was also being almost unnaturally calm. Maybe it was just the effect of the mild tranquilizer Sue had been taking. *If that were me, I would be plotting Jess's murder about now,* Elizabeth acknowledged. But Sue was being more than decent and forgiving.

"You don't have to worry about me," Jessica said airily, reaching for the salt.

Again Mrs. Wakefield put a hand on her husband's arm.

"Jessica, what we're trying to say is that we think it would be a good idea for you and Jeremy not to see each other for a while," her mother said. "Give yourselves time to think this through. Time to cool off. There's always plenty of time later for you to see each other if it's meant to be."

"There's no 'if' about it, Mom," Jessica said evenly. "We know we're meant to be together. It was like that from the moment we met." She made an apologetic face. "Sorry, Sue."

Sue waved her hand and mumbled something, her face flushed bright pink.

"Nevertheless," Mrs. Wakefield continued determinedly, "we are asking you not to see Jeremy for a while."

"How long a while?" was Jessica's surprising response.

"Um." Elizabeth's parents looked taken aback. They had clearly been expecting fireworks, and this calm discussion had thrown their strategy.

"I'm not sure," Mrs. Wakefield said, stalling for time.

"I only asked because it's been almost two weeks since I saw Jeremy. Is that long enough? My feelings for him haven't changed." Jessica popped the last of the roll into her mouth and chewed.

"No, I don't think three weeks is really long enough," Mr. Wakefield said. "I think more like six months would be a good idea."

"I'm sorry, Dad," Jessica said. "But that would be pretty impossible. I mean, since we're engaged and all."

Chapter 7

After what seemed to Elizabeth like aeons of silence, Mr. Wakefield summoned his inner resources and managed to respond with typical lawyerlike succinctness.

"What?" he roared.

Jessica sat calmly eating. "We're engaged, Daddy. Jeremy asked me to marry him, and I said yes. He gave me a ring."

Sue made a small strangled sound, but didn't look up.

Elizabeth was now sitting upright in her chair. She had encouraged Jessica to tell people the truth about her relationship with Jeremy, but somehow she hadn't imagined it would be like this. On the other hand, why had she assumed, knowing Jessica as she did, that it *wouldn't* be like this?

Instinctively she glanced over at Sue, who was staring down at her plate, her face white, her eyes wide. Elizabeth felt a quick pang of sympathy. Jessica was really rubbing salt in her wounds. A fresh wave of worry washed over Elizabeth. Sue's behavior had been erratic enough since the wedding disaster, although in the last week she had finally started looking a little better. Would this latest blow cause her to have a relapse?

Mrs. Wakefield's face looked very much like Sue's, white and shocked, and she was staring at Jessica in horror.

Jessica was cutting up a piece of chicken.

Elizabeth felt a dull sensation of pain in her hands and looked down to see her fingers twisted together so tightly that the knuckles were bloodless. She pulled them apart and put one hand flat on each knee.

"Jessica," Mrs. Wakefield gasped, "please tell me you're joking."

"I'm sorry, Mom." The contriteness in Jessica's voice sounded genuine. "I don't want to hurt you, or anybody, but Jeremy and I are going to be together, and there's nothing anyone can do about it." She made a rueful face and took a bite of her dinner.

"That's where you're wrong, young lady," Mr. Wakefield said grimly. "We're still your parents, and you're still underage, and we can and will take steps to handle this ridiculous and dangerous situation."

"You can't ground me forever, Daddy," Jessica pointed out reasonably. "Jeremy will still be there waiting at the end."

"Jessica, don't you see how unrealistic this is? You're only sixteen, still in high school, and Jeremy is a grown man already out of college. It's true that we can't ground you forever," Mrs. Wakefield said, obviously struggling for self-control, "but there are other options that we can enforce."

Jessica took a sip of milk and looked interested.

"Such as the Milford Academy for Girls, located in Bellevue, Washington. As in 'state,'" Mrs. Wakefield said.

"Oh, yeah. I remember Elizabeth telling me about that," Jessica said calmly.

"It's a very fine school," Mrs. Wakefield said, looking reluctant. "They stress academics and college preparation. We're thinking about making an appointment to talk to the admissions dean. If they find your scholastic qualifications satisfactory, we will seriously consider transferring you there as a boarding student."

"Hmmm," Jessica said, looking thoughtful.

"Jessica—this means no prom this year, no senior year together. You won't live right next door to me. Won't you miss me? Won't you miss your friends?" Elizabeth burst out. It had been bad enough not to have Jessica around for the past several weeks; the thought of getting through the rest of high school without her was totally depressing. This was all Jeremy's fault. He should be able to see how gullible Jessica was—he should have enough sense for both of them. For the hundredth time Elizabeth wondered how her sister could love such a jerk.

"Yes, of course I would miss you, and all my friends," Jessica said slowly. "Of course I want to stay here. But if I have to go to Milford, then I have to go.

90

But it still won't break me and Jeremy up."

"Forgive me for pointing out the obvious, Jessica," Mr. Wakefield said angrily, "but Jeremy hasn't struck me as the most loyal or faithful man that I've ever met. You may imagine that he'll wait for you forever, but two years is a very long time to someone of his age."

Jessica's jaw set stubbornly, but she said nothing.

"Look—let's take some time to cool off, and we can discuss this later. I'm really just too upset to go on right now." Mrs. Wakefield rose and began clearing away plates.

Automatically Elizabeth jumped up to help her. As she was carrying the serving platter into the kitchen, she heard Sue say, "I really wish you two the best, Jessica. No matter what happens."

Jessica's subdued voice answered, "Thanks, Sue. I appreciate it. If there had been any other way—"

"I understand," Sue said quickly. "I just wanted to tell you that Jeremy and I are a closed book. You should just do what you need to do, and don't worry about me at all. I'll probably be heading back to New York soon anyway."

"Thanks," Jessica said gratefully.

Later that night Jessica sat on Elizabeth's bed, her knees drawn up to her chest. After dinner Elizabeth had followed Sue, who had headed for her own room upstairs. The older girl's face was pinched and pale, and her brown eyes held a haunted look. But she had waved Elizabeth away with a brave smile.

"I'm perfectly fine, Elizabeth, really. I already

knew that it was all over between me and Jeremy. What he does now is none of my concern. In fact, I'm glad that he has definite plans—it makes things that much more final. Now I can really start planning how to get on with the rest of my life." Reluctantly, Elizabeth had left Sue in her room.

"How serious do you think Mom and Dad are about boarding school?" Jessica asked now.

Elizabeth could tell that the scene at dinner, especially her father's accusation of Jeremy's untrustworthiness, had rocked Jessica, though typically, she wasn't going to admit it to anyone. Thoughtfully, Elizabeth answered, "I think they're pretty serious, Jess. I've never seen them like this before. For the first time in their lives I think they're actually embarrassed by what's happening. Not to mention totally concerned about you. They don't want you to get hurt, and neither do I." Blue-green eyes met identical blue-green eyes. *How can I make her see? What can I say to show her that this whole thing is a mistake?*

Jessica nodded, looking blankly out the window at the dark night sky.

"Jess, I have something to tell you," Elizabeth said carefully. She knew that the wrong approach could just send Jessica deeper under Jeremy's spell. "I meant to tell you sooner, but there hasn't been a chance. Mom got a letter from Nancy Gibbons's lawyers."

"Sue's mom?"

"Right. Apparently Mrs. Gibbons had made provisions for Mom to inherit all of Sue's money if Sue and Jeremy got married."

"Sue's money? What money? Jeremy's never mentioned anything about Sue having money," Jessica said, looking perplexed.

Elizabeth explained about what Sue had told her and Enid about her MealQuick inheritance.

Jessica whistled. "Are we talking more than a couple million?" she asked, sounding excited. She unfolded her legs on the bed and crossed them. "And Mom is supposed to get it? Oh my God! This is too good to be true. Jeremy and I . . ."

"You aren't listening, Jessica," Elizabeth said. "Mom was to get the money *only* if Sue and Jeremy had gone ahead and gotten married. But since they broke up, she doesn't. If Sue and Jeremy stay broken up for two months, Sue will get everything."

Jessica frowned. "Wait—what you're telling me is that since I stopped the wedding, I prevented Mom from becoming an heiress?" One eyebrow quirked. "And us from becoming heiressettes?"

Elizabeth nodded. "Bingo. Now all Sue has to do is not see Jeremy for another few weeks, and she gets the money her mother intended. The whole MealQuick fortune. And of course we know that Sue and Jeremy won't be seeing each other," she added dryly.

"Gosh, I didn't know," Jessica said wonderingly.

"Regretting having Jeremy instead of the money?" Elizabeth asked with mild sarcasm.

"Of course not!" Jessica shook her head. "Of course I'd rather have Jeremy. There's no question about it. No matter what. Jeremy is all I need," she said a little too loudly. "Sue can keep her money.

93

Maybe it'll help console her for losing the most fabulous man ever born."

Elizabeth was quiet for a moment, weighing her options. *I better just go for it,* she decided. "Jessica—I just had a thought. It may be way off base, but just hear me out. Say Jeremy meets Sue. You've said, actually, that he's said himself he was never in love with her. So what was the attraction? Why did he propose?"

Jessica sighed. "I told you, Liz. He felt sorry for her. She threw herself at him."

"OK." Elizabeth nodded. "What if Sue had another attribute that made her very attractive to him? Like money, for example. Lots and lots of money. And her mother was already very ill."

For a moment Jessica looked confused. Then her eyes widened and an angry expression crossed her face. "Elizabeth Wakefield! I can't believe how your mind works! That's the most hateful—"

Holding up her hands placatingly, Elizabeth broke in. "I'm not saying he's a gold digger." *Though he obviously is.* "I'm just saying maybe he thought he could do a lot of good with the money. Maybe Sue herself suggested just that. The point I'm trying to make is that they were engaged when Sue had money, and they weren't engaged when she didn't."

"You forget, Liz," Jessica said coldly, her eyes flashing, "that I stopped the wedding. Not Jeremy. He would have gone through with it—even though she had no money then. But *I* stopped it."

Elizabeth nodded calmly. "And Jeremy let you," she pointed out. "He was relieved about it."

Her sister stood up and strode angrily to the door. "I don't have to listen to this," Jessica said. "You're just upset because Todd is such a loser and Jeremy is so fabulous."

"I'm just upset because I'm wondering what Jeremy will do to *you* once he learns *you* don't have the money, either," Elizabeth said doggedly.

"Oh!" With a final outraged squeak Jessica slammed out of Elizabeth's room.

Lying back on her bed, Elizabeth pressed a hand over her eyes. She was trying to do what she could to save Jessica, but Jessica wasn't making it easy.

"Winston, honestly, don't worry about it." Maria came to stand next to Winston in front of the full-length mirror in his room. "OK, so it's a little shorter than usual. Just let it alone and let it grow back. I bet in two weeks it'll look like it used to." She smiled encouragingly and patted him on the arm. Poor guy. He was taking it pretty hard. She had to reassure him.

Winston sighed, then turned to the left and to the right. "It's going to take longer than two weeks, Maria. Maybe by Christmas . . ."

Maria laughed and turned him to face her. Stretching up on her tiptoes, she kissed him gently on the mouth. He smiled down at her. Taking her in his arms, he kissed her again.

"I guess you'll just have to be beautiful enough for both of us," he said, rubbing his nose against hers. "You won't be too ashamed of me, looking like this?"

"Oh, please. Don't be silly. I could never be ashamed of you," Maria said loyally. She maneuvered him over to his desk chair and pushed him down on it gently. Then she sat on his lap, with her arm around his shoulders. She nibbled his ear, and he closed his eyes.

"Mmmm," he said.

"I mean," she whispered into his ear, "it's not like you're growing a disgusting pseudo-mustache, like Todd." True, she wasn't crazy about Winston's new look—in fact, she would be thrilled when his hair grew out again. But one glance at Todd had convinced her she was definitely better off than Elizabeth.

Winston broke out into laughter, and Maria joined in. They kissed again.

Robby Goodman sat by the large swimming pool that separated the main mansion from his father's cottage. His dad was inside, watching the late news, but Robby had wanted to be alone.

He was still upset about the argument he'd had with Lila. Dammit, he loved her. She was the best thing that had ever happened to him. But she was just too used to getting her own way. Usually almost everything she did was fine with him. He liked the fact that she was forceful and worldly. She always knew the best places to go and the best things to do. And since she had realized he didn't have much money, she had been generous and even sensitive about paying for some of their dates.

Their relationship meant a lot to him. It was a total drag feeling angry at her, knowing she was angry at him. On the other hand, how could he let her do this? She simply couldn't make such a huge decision without telling him about it. Robby frowned. He had hidden the college envelope in his room where his father wouldn't see it. What would his dad think, if Robby accepted such an expensive gift from Lila? It was almost like being a kept man, like a gigolo or something. Robby stifled a laugh. Maybe it wasn't exactly like that, but . . .

No, he decided. He had done the right thing in refusing. He knew she meant well, but she was out of line here. He just hoped she got over it pretty soon so they could get back together. He really missed her.

It was late, very late. Jessica lay in her bed, where she had been tossing and turning for hours. Her nightgown was twisted up around her knees. For the thousandth time she looked at the sparkly ring on her left hand. She always wore it when she was alone in her room, or when she was at school. But not in front of her parents or Sue.

The shadows flitted around her room. She looked at the clock again. Finally she came to a decision.

After opening her bedroom door very slowly, she listened for any sounds that would indicate someone else was awake. But the entire Wakefield house was silent and dark. Jessica crept down the hallway to the stairs, the red Spanish tiles cool and smooth beneath her bare feet.

She avoided the stair that squeaked, seventh from the bottom. Once downstairs she went down the hallway to the den, and through that to her father's small study. Often he brought work home from the office, and this small paneled room that had once been a pantry off the kitchen had been refitted to give him privacy.

Jessica shut the door very quietly, then made her way to the desk. She didn't turn on a light; she didn't need to. Instead she patted around on the desk for the phone and lifted it into her lap as she sat on a leather ottoman.

In her hand was a crumpled scrap of paper, and she unfolded it to read the phone number in the slanting crack of bright moonlight that was filtering in through the curtains. Her hand trembling, she carefully punched in Lila's calling-card number so this call wouldn't show up on her own phone bill. She would pay Lila back later. Then she dialed the number Jeremy had given her.

The phone rang once, twice. No one answered. Jessica wondered what time it was in Costa Rica. Jeremy had explained the time difference, but the details had gone out of her head. She hoped she wasn't waking up his roommate. After six rings Jessica began to feel desperation creeping up her spine to tighten the muscles at the back of her neck. It must be late there—where was Jeremy?

Jessica almost screamed in relief when she heard the phone being picked up on the other end.

"Jeremy?" she cried, happiness flooding through her.

"Uh-uh. You must have the wrong—oh. You want Jeremy?" the male, slightly Spanish-accented voice asked.

"Yes. Yes, I have to speak to Jeremy," Jessica said urgently.

"Uh, he isn't here right now. He, uh, had to run an errand. But I'll tell him you called, and he'll call you back. OK?"

Tears of frustration sprang to Jessica's eyes. It seemed as if Jeremy was never there when she called, although she had called only twice before, from Lila's house. And she really, really had to talk to him right now—she needed to talk to him about the boarding school, and Sue's money, and everything. . . . "Yeah, OK," she said wearily. "Could you please tell him that Jessica called? Jessica."

"Sure, no prob," Jeremy's roommate answered. "I'll tell him."

After hanging up the phone and replacing it on her father's desk, Jessica crept back upstairs to her own room. Once inside, she threw herself down on her bed, burying her face in her pillow. Then she started to cry.

Jeremy lay on his small single bed, the wrinkled sheets pushed to one side. It was a warm, muggy night, and moonlight poured in through the thin curtain at the small window. One hand held a cigarette, and smoke curled lazily up toward the cinder-block ceiling of his room. An ashtray sat on his chest.

On the rickety bedside table were two framed photographs. One was a smiling, brown-eyed, brown-haired girl with a gently rounded face and fair skin. One was a girl with lightly tanned smooth skin, long blond hair, and beautiful, almond-shaped, blue-green eyes.

Jeremy could make out the two girls' features in

the moonlight. Sue's was more of a traditional, English-type prettiness, he mused, while Jessica's was definitely a more modern, American-rose type of beauty. He smiled at both of them, then stubbed out the cigarette in the ashtray.

"I'll see you soon, sweetheart," he whispered, putting the ashtray on the bedside table. Then he jumped a little when the phone rang, and he laughed at his skittishness.

"Yeah?"

"Jeremy, that girl called. She wants you to call her." It wasn't the first time his friend Juan had had to pass on a message.

"OK, thanks, man." Jeremy hung up the phone, then sat on the edge of his bed, looking at his hands.

Chapter 8

"Please pass the juice," Alice Wakefield said coolly the next morning. The four Wakefields were sitting in their usual places around the breakfast table, but that was the only thing normal about this Friday morning.

Jessica silently passed the pitcher of orange juice to her mother. *Thank God it's Friday.* As often as she had thought that through the years, never had she meant it more than today. She had been home only one day, and already she was ready to go back to Lila's. True, it was nice to be home among all her own things, and she was glad to be close to Elizabeth again, but after last night's scene . . . She wondered if anyone she knew could possibly be having harder teenage years than she was. No way.

Jeremy hadn't called back last night, though Jessica had waited anxiously by the phone on her bedside table for what seemed like hours. When she had finally given up and tried to get some sleep, she had made sure both the hall door and the bathroom door to her room were locked. Sue might look as though she were taking it all very well, but one never knew. Better to be safe.

Jessica felt tired, washed-out, and grumpy from lack of sleep and worry. Why hadn't he called back? Where had he been? Ugh. She just wanted to go back to bed for, like, two years. It would be great if she could just sleep until she was eighteen. Then none of this would be a problem. She would just wake up, take off with Jeremy, and never have to deal with any of this again.

"Well, today I'm going to talk to Mr. Collins about my article on the Go Math program," Elizabeth said in an attempt to make conversation. Roger Collins was her English teacher, and also the faculty adviser for *The Oracle*.

"That's nice, honey," Mr. Wakefield said absently.

Elizabeth continued. "I could interview students and get differing opinions."

"Good idea," Mr. Wakefield said, taking a sip of his coffee. "Be nonjudgmental."

"Uh-huh," Elizabeth said.

Jessica turned to the fashion section of the newspaper. "Whoa. Look at these platform shoes."

"It won't be too long before it's fall," Alice Wakefield said. "Maybe later, toward the end of October, we could all drive up north along the coast. Just the four of us." She lowered her voice. "I'm sure Sue will be back in New York by then. Probably throwing herself into her work would be the best thing for her. We could take a long weekend. Carmel would be so pretty then."

"That would be great, Mom," Elizabeth said, nodding.

"If I'm at boarding school, it would be just the three of you," Jessica said diffidently. Her head ached from lack of sleep, and her eyes were red and felt as though they had little grits of sand in them. But she couldn't show she was afraid.

"That's true, Jessica. We'll just have to play it by ear. Well, I better get going," Mr. Wakefield said abruptly. "When I get to the office, I'm going to make an appointment to talk to the dean at Milford. I'll let you know when the meeting is, Jessica, so you can be available."

Jessica didn't say anything. Elizabeth saw her mother's mouth tighten and felt her own stomach knot with anxiety. How much longer could she stand for her family to be in turmoil like this? It was almost as bad as when her parents had agreed to a trial separation, and Mr. Wakefield had moved out to his own apartment for a while.

Mr. Wakefield stood up and carried his plate to the sink.

"Goodness, where's Sue this morning?" Mrs. Wakefield said with artificial brightness, glancing at the clock. "She's been sleeping in lately, but today I think she was planning to go to work at Project Nature in Los Angeles."

"I'll go call her," Elizabeth offered.

"Thanks, honey," her mother said.

Anything to get away from the breakfast table of doom, Elizabeth thought, pounding up the stairs and down the hall to Steven's room. She tapped gently on the door.

103

"Sue? It's Elizabeth." Elizabeth tapped again. *She must still be sleeping.* Elizabeth turned the doorknob. She frowned. The door was locked from the inside. Knocking louder, Elizabeth called, "Sue? It's getting late. Are you going to work today?" She used her fist and knocked louder still, a sense of panic starting to rise in her throat. "Sue! Come on, Sue, open the door!"

A moment later her parents, followed by Jessica, hurried up the stairs.

"What is it, honey? Isn't she answering?" Alice Wakefield asked, her hand at her throat.

Elizabeth shook her head wordlessly.

Mr. Wakefield stepped to the door and pounded on it. The hallway reverberated with the echoing sound. "Sue!" he cried. "Can you hear me? Open this door!"

The Wakefields waited with bated breath as the silent moments ticked past.

"Ned, you don't think—" Mrs. Wakefield began.

"OK, stand back," Mr. Wakefield said in an ominous tone. "I'm going to try to break the door in." Grimly he stepped back a few paces, then seemed to brace himself for the blow.

"Dad! Wait," Jessica said, putting a hand on his arm. "There's a better way. Hang on." She flew down the hallway toward her room.

Seconds later she returned, holding a long, thin hairpin. She straightened it out, leaned over, and carefully worked it into a tiny hole in the middle of the doorknob. Then she fiddled with it for a few moments, her brow wrinkled in concentration. They

104

heard a click, and Jessica popped the door open.

Mr. Wakefield pushed his way into Sue's room. They all crowded around the doorway and peered in.

"She's asleep," Jessica said in relief.

Sue was sprawled across her bed, with one arm flung over her head. She was wearing a nightgown and bathrobe, and one bare foot was sticking out from under the covers. In sleep she looked young and peaceful, almost serene.

"Don't you get it? She's not asleep," Elizabeth cried. She pushed past her mother and ran to the bed. Then she picked up Sue's cold hand and started patting it, hard.

"Sue, come on," she muttered, feeling for a pulse. "Come on."

That's when the rest of the family saw the empty, overturned pill bottle lying on the floor by the bed, and the neatly folded note lying next to it.

Jessica gasped and ran into the room, snatching up the note. While her father began CPR on Sue, Mrs. Wakefield called for an emergency ambulance. Jessica stood there, feeling as though the room, and in fact the whole world, were spinning crazily out of control. As though in a dream, she watched her father begin mouth-to-mouth resuscitation. Dreamily, she unfolded the note and began to read it.

Soon the wailing siren of an ambulance pierced the fog of Jessica's brain, and her mother shoved her out of the way to make room for the emergency medical team. Jessica leaned against the door to Steven's room, the spidery, handwritten words of the note swirling through her brain.

Everyone, please forgive me. I don't want to hurt anyone or cause pain. But with everything that's happened lately, there isn't any point in going on. . . .

As the emergency crew loaded Sue onto a wheeled stretcher, Jessica could only watch helplessly. *This isn't my fault,* she thought. *There's no way this could be my fault. This is definitely not my fault. My loving Jeremy could never have caused such pain.* But there was really no way to know. Not now.

"Oh. My. God," Enid said, staring at Elizabeth. It was after lunch on Friday, and they were walking to their new Go Math class together. "So what happened? Is she—"

"No," Elizabeth said, pushing open the door to their classroom. "She's going to be OK. But we had to call an ambulance, and then we all rushed to the hospital, and Sue had her stomach pumped."

"Good grief, I just can't believe it," Enid said. "Poor Sue. So she had taken all her tranquilizers? That's so awful. What does Jessica have to say about it?"

Elizabeth had filled Enid in on all the events of the previous night, when Jessica had announced her engagement.

"Not a lot. She's pretty shaken up." Elizabeth and Enid found seats next to each other toward the back of class. "I mean, I know she usually acts for selfish reasons, but I'm sure she never intended for Sue to try to commit suicide," she finished in a whisper. "She was crying in the waiting room."

"Whoa." Enid shook her head. "The whole thing

is just so unbelievable. I mean, I knew Sue was majorly upset, but I figured that with time, she'd just get over it."

Elizabeth nodded. "Yeah. I guess we all did."

"Good afternoon, class."

Elizabeth and Enid looked up. They had been so engrossed in talking that they hadn't noticed the new teacher standing at the front of the classroom. He was tall, in his midthirties, Elizabeth guessed, and had wavy chestnut hair and warm brown eyes. He didn't look too much like a sexist pig, she thought.

"My name is Mr. Barton, and I'll be your teacher during our Go Math experiment," he said. "I've been trained specifically to teach these new classes." He smiled at everyone.

Elizabeth looked around and saw that she knew most of the girls in the classroom. Penny Ayala was sitting a few seats away, and so was Olivia Davidson, Maria Santelli, Caroline Pearce, Claire Middleton, and Grace Oliver. The shy girl, Molly Adams, was sitting in the back row, and there were several girls whom Elizabeth recognized but had never talked to.

"The point of this program," Mr. Barton continued, "is equality—though it may not seem that way to you now. In fact, some of you may feel angry about this program, as though female students are being singled out as inferior, or dumber in some way than male students."

Elizabeth sat up in surprise. She did feel that way.

"But I'd like to reassure you that this isn't the case at all." Mr. Barton walked over to his desk and picked up a textbook. "These classes are based on the fact that there are inescapable, fundamental *social* differences between adolescent males and females. Some of you may have noticed this," he said with a grin.

Several of the girls in class laughed, and Elizabeth couldn't help smiling.

"Let me say it again. There are *social* differences. Not intellectual. Not in regards to intelligence. Not in terms of ability to learn. Not in natural abilities, such as a predisposition toward being good in English or being good in math. But social."

Elizabeth shot Enid a look that said, *Hmmm.*

Enid tapped the edge of her notebook. Elizabeth glanced down and saw that Enid had written "Hunk" in the margin. Elizabeth stifled a giggle. Mr. Barton *was* kind of good-looking, for a teacher.

"Let's talk some more about what that means," the teacher said, walking over to the blackboard.

Elizabeth opened her notebook and started taking notes. This was certainly going to affect the slant of her *Oracle* article.

"You're kidding me. You have got to be kidding," Lila said, opening her purse and taking out her lip gloss.

"I wish I was," Jessica groaned. The two girls had ducked into a bathroom to talk for a moment between classes.

"It was amazingly awful, Li," Jessica continued, leaning against a sink. "I was so afraid that she was going to die. I kept thinking how stupid it was—killing yourself because you broke up with your fiancé.

It just seemed so wrong, so pointless. Sue is only eighteen. She has plenty of time to find someone else."

Lila looked at Jessica in the mirror. "She didn't break up with him; he dumped her, very publicly, in the middle of their *wedding*." She took out her hairbrush and leaned over, letting her long brown hair cascade almost to the floor.

Jessica flushed. "So you think it's my fault that Sue tried to commit suicide?"

"I didn't say that," Lila mumbled, still bent over. She brushed her hair vigorously. "I agree with you that Jeremy never would have carried on with you the way he did if their relationship hadn't been rocky anyway. But Sue did take a major blow over it, and then when she found out you two were engaged, it must have just sent her over the edge." Lila straightened up, and her hair poufed out around her like a cloud.

"Oh, that's an attractive look," Jessica said sarcastically. "You look like you live in Holly-weird."

Lila snickered and started brushing her hair flat again. "So what's the news on her, anyway? Is she going to be OK?" She stopped brushing, her face serious. "I mean, she's not going to be brain damaged or anything, is she?"

Jessica shook her head. The class bell rang, but they both ignored it. "No. The doctor said she's going to be fine. She didn't actually take that much. In fact, he said if he had realized how little she had taken, he wouldn't have pumped her stomach. But he did it at the time just to be on the safe side."

"Bleah." Lila made a face. "Is she going to stay in the hospital for a while?"

"Uh-uh. I think Mom and Dad are bringing her home late this afternoon. But she'll have to take it easy for a couple of days. I asked Mom if I should stay at your house for a while, but she said no. Something about how we all have to work through it together."

"Well, you're welcome if you change your mind."

"Thanks. And how are things with the Rob-ster?"

"Don't ask. We're both playing it very cool. I haven't seen him in days." With one last look in the mirror, Lila gathered up her things and headed out of the rest room. Jessica sighed and followed her.

A few minutes later in comparative-lit class, Jessica saw a note sliding onto her desk from Amy Sutton, who sat in front of her. Very quietly she unfolded it and read it. It said, "This is so boring. The only thing keeping me going is looking forward to video club right after this. You should have joined."

Jessica wrote, "That's all I need, another commitment taking up my time and energy. Just doing cheerleading is enough," and passed the note back to Amy.

It was several minutes before Amy could reply. She wrote, "Well, can you at least come see my video when it's all done? We're going to hold a public screening. I'll let you know when."

Smiling, Jessica wrote, "Sure," and slipped the note back to her friend. She had been hearing about all the far-out films the artsy video-club crowd was planning. Amy was working on a black-and-white "mood piece" about Sweet Valley, trying to show a different side of the familiar city. And Winston had been telling them about his documentary on all the best places to kiss in Sweet Valley. It would be nice to have something light and normal to look forward to, Jessica decided. Not to mention the fact that it would get her out of the house and away from Sue for a while.

"Elizabeth, what's wrong with you? It's Saturday night." Todd pulled back and sat away from Elizabeth on the couch in the Wakefield family room. It seemed as though she had been moody for weeks, he thought. Now she didn't even want to go out. They always went out on Saturday.

Elizabeth looked away. "I don't know, Todd. I just don't feel like going anywhere, that's all. Can't we just stay here? We could watch a movie, eat some popcorn . . ."

Todd sighed. "Liz, we did that last weekend. I mean, I like being here OK, but it's not exactly private. Who knows when your folks would come in, or Jessica, or Sue?"

Elizabeth turned her blue-green eyes to his. "A movie or the Dairi Burger isn't exactly private, either," she pointed out.

Todd felt a twinge of frustration. "No, but it's not under your parents' watchful eyes. I want to go out, see people, do stuff." He forced a laugh. "God, it's like you don't want to be seen in public with me or something." He laughed again.

Elizabeth flushed and looked away.

Todd sighed and started tapping his foot against the floor. "How's your new girls-only math class?" he asked, deciding to steer toward safer ground.

"Well, it's different," Elizabeth said, showing more animation than she had all evening. "I still think it's sexist, but yesterday Mr. Barton, our teacher, was explaining some of the reasoning behind it, and it was interesting. I'm still going to write my article, but I might wait awhile, see how the class shapes up. Mr. Collins said that they're doing the experiment in some of the elementary schools, too. I'd be interested in visiting some of them, talking to the students. See what they think about it." She finished, the excited expression on her face making her look really pretty, Todd thought.

He smiled at her. "I'm glad that it's giving you a story you can sink your teeth into." He slid over next to her and put his arm around her shoulders. She didn't smile and cuddle up next to him the way she usually did.

"How's Sue doing?" he asked, stroking the soft skin of her shoulder.

"OK. She keeps apologizing for it—for causing us trouble. Can you imagine? I just feel so sorry for her." Elizabeth leaned back into Todd's arm. "Mom made her stay in bed all day today, but she'll probably get up tomorrow. And you know what? We called her stepfather from the hospital, just to let him know what had happened. He was out of town on business, and when he finally called back, he said that if everything was under control, he didn't see a need to come to California. I couldn't believe it. I mean, I know they're not related by blood, but he was married to her mother for eight years. He watched Sue grow up. And he didn't feel a need to come see her! No wonder Sue feels so alone and desperate," Elizabeth finished in indignation. She snuggled closer to Todd and rested her head on his shoulder.

Finally. Todd put his other arm around her and stroked the hair off her face. She closed her eyes and smiled.

Yes. Keep it going, Wilkins. She's relaxing.

"It's a good thing she has you to be so supportive," Todd murmured, stroking her hair. "She's really lucky."

Elizabeth turned to face him a little, her eyes still closed.

"Where are your parents?" Todd whispered.

"Upstairs," Elizabeth said dreamily.

And we know Sue is out of commission. "And Jessica?"

"She went out with Lila, I think."

Yes! Todd leaned over very slowly and brushed his lips against Elizabeth's hair. It was so soft, so silky. "I love your hair," he said softly. "Don't ever cut it. Let it get really long, OK?"

What was that? Did she stiffen up? Maintaining constant pressure with the hand rubbing Elizabeth's back, Todd shifted a little bit on the couch. There. Now if he could just get her knee to unbend a little . . .

Ahhh. Yes. Elizabeth had curled both arms around his neck and leaned back against the couch. He bent over her, changing their angle slightly, then lowered his lips to hers. Gently he kissed her, thinking about how much he had missed her lately. True, they saw each other every day at school, but it wasn't like the summer, when they could spend time together practically whenever they wanted. He increased the pressure of the kiss, tightening his arms around her.

She always smells so good. Why is that? She was holding him close now, and his breath started coming faster. They had really had some ups and downs, and there were times when he felt he hardly knew her, or knew her too well. But always, as soon as he kissed her, his fears disappeared, and everything seemed all right again.

He noticed that Elizabeth was pushing against his chest. *Now what?*

"Todd—hold on. Let me get some air." Elizabeth opened her eyes and sat up, then seemed to rub her hand across her mouth. She moved an inch away from him on the couch and jumped up. "How about some soda?" she asked brightly. "I'll make us some microwave popcorn. Back in a jiff."

Todd watched in exasperation as she went into the kitchen. *What is the matter with that girl?* Usually she couldn't wait to be alone with him. Todd rolled his eyes and flopped back against the couch. *Women,* he mused, stroking his fuzzy mustache despondently. He twisted one end of it so that it curled up a little, then the other. It was really coming along, he thought proudly. *I just don't understand her.*

Chapter 9

On Wednesday morning at school Jessica ran into Elizabeth at their lockers, which were next to each other.

"Hi, Liz," Jessica said, touching up her lip gloss in the mirror she had hung inside her locker door. "I hate not being in math class with you." Jessica was still in a boy-girl algebra II course. "Besides homeroom and lunch, we don't have any classes together."

"You mean besides history, English, and French?" Elizabeth said dryly, taking out her books for her morning classes.

Jessica turned to face her. "Well, besides those. It's math I miss you in." She smiled sweetly at her twin.

"Yeah, and I know why," Elizabeth returned tolerantly. "But you'll find some poor sap to copy off of."

Jessica's eyebrows rose. "You wound me, you really do."

Elizabeth grinned at her. "You seem chipper this morning."

Beaming, Jessica took out some books at random and slammed her locker door. "My love called last night. Heaven, I'm in heaven," she sang. She waved her ring under Elizabeth's nose.

"Oh, please," Elizabeth groaned. Her face sobered. "Did you tell him about Sue?"

Jessica's face fell also. She bit her lip. "No, I didn't. I just said that she was still down, but doing OK. I didn't know what to tell him, Liz," she said to Elizabeth's accusing expression.

"Uh-huh. But, Jess, don't you think he has a right to—"

"Jessica, Jessica, Jessica." Bruce Patman walked up to them in the hall, his usual cocky grin firmly in place. The Patmans were one of the wealthiest families in Sweet Valley, and Bruce was one of the best-looking boys in the senior class. Jessica and Elizabeth had known him since grade school. Most people thought of him as totally obnoxious, spoiled, and arrogant, and they were right. But Elizabeth knew that he was genuinely sweet to his girlfriend, Pamela Robertson, and that he did have a softer, more vulnerable side to him that rarely showed. She had seen it briefly several months earlier, when she and Jessica had helped him save his parents' marriage.

Now he leaned against their lockers, smirking down at them. "Jessica, Jessica, Jessica," he said again.

"That's right—you've got one of us. And do you remember *her* name?" Jessica asked nastily, pointing to Elizabeth. Bruce ignored it.

116

"Jessica, you little home wrecker, you. You just can't keep your hands to yourself, can you?"

"If I remember correctly, you like it when I can't keep my hands to myself." Jessica slammed her locker shut and stood glaring at him.

Bruce's jaw tightened at her mention of their brief and ancient history. "Yeah, yeah. But to go after a married man, Jess. That seems low—even for you. If I had known about it, I never would have let myself get sucked in."

Last month, when Jeremy had still been determined to go ahead with the wedding, Jessica had gotten Bruce to agree to be her "boyfriend" for one evening. It had succeeded in making Jeremy jealous.

"Oh, please," Jessica said. "You liked it. And you certainly ate like a pig."

"Everyone knows that you broke up their wedding," Bruce continued, ignoring her comment.

"Bruce, it was almost a month ago. And you're just hassling me about it now? You're slipping," Jessica said snidely. "And for your information, there was no home to wreck. They weren't married yet. I may have ruined the wedding, but I didn't break up a marriage. Not that it's any of your business." Eyes narrowed, Jessica flung her purse on top of her books and stalked down the hall. "Catch you later, Liz," she called over her shoulder.

"Later, Jess," Elizabeth called, glancing at Bruce and shrugging her shoulders helplessly.

His eyes met hers, and for one uncomfortable second Elizabeth flashed on a memory of herself and Bruce locked in an embrace in the Wakefields' kitchen. She wished for the thousandth time that Todd hadn't grown his revolting mustache.

"Does the phrase 'evil twin' mean anything to you?" Bruce asked humorlessly, jerking his head toward where Jessica had disappeared down the hall. "I can't believe you two are related."

Elizabeth met his gaze. "Jessica and I do have *some* things in common," she reminded him pointedly.

He flushed. "Geez, I guess it's my day to catch it from both Wakefields. Let me go to trig class so I can relax."

Elizabeth gave him a half smile, then headed to her own class. Sometimes she couldn't help sticking up for Jessica. It must be genetic or something.

"I must say, I feel sorry for Maria," Lila said in a low voice during lunch on Wednesday. "Ol' Winston is looking more and more like Michael Jordan every day." She took a french fry and drenched it in ketchup.

"Yeah. Except he isn't tall. Or sexy. Or black. Or a basketball player." Amy Sutton took a long sip of her diet soda.

Lila tittered. "I guess it's just the hair, then."

"Well, personally, I feel sorrier for my own dear sister. I mean, just look at Todd," Jessica said, pointing a fork to where Todd was standing in the lunch line. "Let's face it—he's trying to look like Tom Selleck, but he's coming out like Gene Shalit."

The girls at her table laughed.

"Who wants to look like Tom Selleck, anyway? He's ancient. Todd should be trying for Jason

Windsong," Sandy Bacon said. Jason Windsong was a television actor with a sexy mustache.

"Yeah, right," Jessica said sarcastically. Then her eyes took on a dreamy look. "I'm glad Jeremy doesn't have a mustache," she said. "I like being able to see his mouth." She took a suggestive bite of fruit cocktail.

Her friends groaned.

"Have you heard from him lately?" Amy asked. "How long has he been gone now?"

"Weeks! But he should be home pretty soon," Jessica said. Actually, she had no idea when he was coming back. He hadn't given her a date. "He's pretty busy, though. He's working really hard in Costa Rica. Every time I call him, he's out in the field, doing research. But he always calls me right back. I bet he comes home with a great tan. And then we can start really planning the wedding." She smiled smugly.

"Despite the fact that it's two years away," Sandy said tolerantly. "How about you, Lila? Care to give us vicarious thrills with your own love life for a while?"

Lila looked despondent. "My love life is a mess. I still haven't seen Robby since the business-school fiasco. Maybe I should let it drop, but I can't help feeling mad at him for not going, and he can't help feeling mad that I want him to go. Not to mention all the tuition money I threw away." She grimaced. "The gallery is still planning his opening, but he hasn't asked me to go yet. I don't know what's going to happen." She leaned forward and looked at her friends earnestly. "I mean, I adore Robby—it's like he's made

119

for me. But I can't just watch him throw away his talent and success because he doesn't know how to handle money, can I? How will he ever get ahead? Does he expect me to be there to bail him out for the rest of his life?" Her brown eyes looked troubled.

Jessica offered her a slice of apple. "You were just looking out for him," she agreed.

"Yeah," Lila said. "He just doesn't want me to."

"What are we going to do?" Maria Santelli asked in a low whisper. She was sitting across from Elizabeth at their usual table in the cafeteria.

Elizabeth groaned. "I don't know," she admitted. "At least you have the consolation that Winston's hair will grow back, and it's not his fault that he looks kind of lame right now. Todd is doing it by *choice*. I don't know when he's going to come to his senses. I can hardly bear to look at him." Feeling depressed, she hung her head low over her turkey sandwich.

"Maybe Winston ought to get a wig," Maria said thoughtfully. She looked up, suddenly indignant. "And the worst thing is, he's gone back twice to get it fixed. By the same guy! I keep telling him, 'Winston, try somebody new. Don't go back to the guy who butchered your hair in the first place.' But every time he goes back, he winds up getting the same old man. And now look at him. He has a crew cut. More than a crew cut." Maria shook her head disgustedly.

Elizabeth nodded in commiseration. Just then Todd breezed up, holding his lunch tray. He plopped it down next to Elizabeth, then leaned over and kissed her cheek, rubbing his mustache lovingly against her. "Not too scratchy anymore, right, babe? 'Cause it's getting longer." He grinned proudly.

I'm going to hurl, Elizabeth thought drearily.

Sue glanced at the clock above the stove in the Wakefield kitchen. Almost three thirty. Jessica and Elizabeth could be home at any minute. Putting down her magazine, she went to the front door and checked to see if the mail had come.

There was a small table in the hallway, and Sue piled the mail neatly there. Mr. and Mrs. Wakefield had their own stack, Elizabeth had gotten a new computer magazine, and Jessica had received her latest issue of *Hollywood Madness.* Jessica also had a postcard from Costa Rica. Sue read it and smiled.

She took her own letter with its California postmark and went up to her room to read it in private.

"OK, now, let's look at what we have for the next issue," Mr. Collins said. It was after school on Wednesday, and Elizabeth was in the *Oracle* staff room. Mr. Collins looked at a list in his hand. "Tina, you were going to do a photo essay on new faces at Sweet Valley High. And, Olivia, you were going to write an accompanying article."

"Right," Olivia confirmed. "I think Tina and I are both about ready. We'll give the photos and my copy disk to Andy Jenkins tomorrow." Tina Ayala was the staff photographer for the newspaper, and Andy was taking over the job of typesetting and layout.

"Good," Mr. Collins said. "I see we also have a

feature planned about all the different extracurricular activities, Cheryl. Don't forget to mention that *The Oracle* is always looking for new members."

"I won't," Cheryl Thomas replied. Cheryl was Elizabeth's next-door neighbor, and the stepsister of Annie Whitman, who was on the cheerleading squad with Jessica. Her pretty, dark-skinned face crinkled into a smile. "And I won't put in the Dairi Burger as an extracurricular activity, either."

Everyone laughed.

"Maybe you should," Andy said jokingly.

"Elizabeth? You were going to do something about the Go Math classes. At our last meeting you were all burned up about the implied sexism. What have you done with that so far?"

Elizabeth hesitated. Mr. Collins was one of the first people she had gone to about the Go Math program. She had promised him an exposé that would stop the program in its tracks. He had cautioned her to be careful and get all the facts.

"Well—I've realized that it's more complicated than I thought," she admitted. "It's not just about sexism, or girls being inferior. Actually," she said, "I've been in the class less than a week, but I can already see big changes in some of the students. I have a short, unbiased piece ready for the paper—just explaining about the program, what it is, who originated it, and so on. But I wanted to make it into a weekly series—tracking the progress of the students, talking about what's happening at the grade-school level, putting in some statistics. That kind of thing."

"OK," Mr. Collins agreed. "That sounds good. Maybe Andy can come up with some graphs or charts that could accompany your article."

"No prob," Andy said, making a note to himself.

"Now, what's next?" Mr. Collins asked.

The staff of the newspaper continued to go down their schedule, planning what features to use on the first page and how the rest of the paper should be laid out. Elizabeth sat in her chair, half listening to the discussion and half lost in her own thoughts. Today in math class Molly Adams had actually volunteered an answer. She had gotten it right. Maria Santelli had answered another problem incorrectly, but no one had made fun of her or yelled out the right answer. The whole atmosphere of class was very different. Elizabeth needed to think about it.

It was a very hot day. Jeremy wiped the sweat from his brow and took another sip of his beer. Twenty feet in front of him, crystal-blue waves crashed rhythmically on the shore. Jeremy lay back in his folding chair and adjusted the sunglasses on his nose. He had been on the phone all morning, doing research, making plans. He deserved a little break. Not too long from now he would be going back to New York to wrap things up. He had a lot to take care of before then.

Behind him the palm trees swayed in the fresh ocean breeze. Jeremy closed his eyes and sighed. In the last month things had gotten very sticky, and they were bound to be stickier before everything was straightened out. But not too long from now, he would be in the right place with the right person. He just had to look forward to that.

Right after school on Friday, Mrs. Wakefield picked up Jessica. It was a short drive downtown to Mr. Wakefield's law office.

Mrs. Wakefield turned to smile brittlely at Jessica. "Are you nervous, sweetheart?"

Jessica took a slow breath. With all the strength she had in her, she said calmly, "No. Why should I be?"

Her mother looked away for a moment, pressing her lips together. "Jessica—you understand that we're not trying to get rid of you. You're our daughter and we love you. We'll always love you no matter what. But we're very worried about you. We're worried about the decisions you've been making lately. This whole thing with Jeremy and Sue—it doesn't seem like you."

Jessica sat patiently, trying to remain calm, staring out her window. In her mind she pictured getting up at six o'clock every morning to the sound of a gong. She and a hundred other girls would roll out of their white iron beds in a huge cavernlike room. She would gently kiss Jeremy's picture, then hide it under her pillow again before making her bed with military corners.

Since there was no heat, even in winter, she and her dormmates would fight about who got to use the small amount of warm, not hot, water available. Jessica pictured herself winning. After dressing in rough, ugly wool dresses that did nothing for their figures or coloring, she and her dormmates would line up to go to the cafeteria, a grim place of gray-painted cinder blocks. After their usual cold gruel, the Klaxon would sound again, signaling them for their early-morning five-mile hike through freezing rain . . . and yet, through it all, Jeremy's love would warm her, sustain her, help her get through. She would call him every month, her one allotted phone call to the outside world. But it would all be worth it, because at graduation he would be there, smiling, ready to take her away forever. . . .

"Here we are." Mrs. Wakefield opened her car door, and they went upstairs to Mr. Wakefield's office.

He was waiting for them, and when Jessica entered his office, she saw an older woman wearing an olive-green business suit.

"Jessica, this is Ms. Turner. She's the admissions dean at Milford," Mr. Wakefield introduced them. "Ms. Turner, this is our daughter, Jessica."

Jessica stepped forward and shook the woman's hand.

"Hello, Jessica," Ms. Turner said pleasantly. "It's so nice to meet you."

Jessica smiled tightly.

Chapter 10

It was late. Jessica lay quietly in her room in the dark, watching the shifting shadows and patterns of light on the ceiling. Slowly she traced the shapes of leaves that the streetlight outside had thrown onto her wall. She looked at the digital clock by her bed. Past midnight.

Then she heard it: the faint click that the phone made in the second before it was about to ring. With practice Jessica had gotten so that she could snatch up the handset before the ringer actually had time to start.

"Hello?" she whispered.

"Jess, it's me," came Jeremy's warm, comforting voice.

Breathing a sigh of relief, Jessica sank back into her pillows, a feeling of happiness stealing over her.

"Hi," she said lovingly. "How are you? I haven't talked to you in, oh, about three days." She smiled into the darkness.

Jeremy chuckled. "It seems like years since I saw you. Is everything OK there?"

"No," Jessica said firmly. "Nothing is OK without you. Jeremy, it's been almost five weeks. When are you coming back?"

Jeremy groaned. "Soon, honey. Things down here have gotten more complicated. One of the other field researchers was called back to New York suddenly, and I've had to take over his project. I'm sorry. It looks like it's going to be another week or two."

"Oh, Jeremy! I can't stand it. You've been gone for so long. Things keep happening here, and you're not here, and I just need to see you." Jessica felt near tears. Suddenly she remembered the premonition she'd had at the airport the day she dropped him off. She'd felt almost sick with dread, as though she would never see him again, that he wouldn't come back, that he would fall in love with someone else. Intellectually she didn't believe that; emotionally she felt frantic, neglected, and practically hysterical.

"I'm sorry, honey, really I am. If there was any way I could get out of it, I would. But I can't just take off—I have a job to do. Remember, I'm only doing this so that they'll transfer me to Los Angeles, so I can be near you."

Instantly Jessica felt guilty. "I know. It's just that it's so hard sometimes."

"I know. But I'll be back soon. And listen, I have a surprise for you. The L.A. chapter of Project Nature has their own cabin, in a nature preserve about half an hour from Sweet Valley. They're throwing a big

127

Halloween party there, and they've said I can invite anyone I want."

"A Halloween party?"

"Yeah. I thought it would be fun to ask everyone we know—all your friends from school, and Robby Goodman, and some of my other friends from PN are going to come. We'll make it a total blowout. How does that sound?"

Jessica hesitated, twisting the phone cord around her finger. "It sounds fun, but Halloween is so far away. Are you saying I won't see you until then?" She took a deep breath, trying not to sound whiny and immature.

"I just don't know, Jess. It could be next week, it could be a couple of weeks from now. I just have to finish everything up here. You know that I would be with you if I could. I really miss you," he said huskily.

"I miss you, too," Jessica said, feeling very sorry for herself. What was the point of having a fabulous boyfriend if she never got to see him? "I wish you could hold me."

"Mmmm," Jeremy said, his voice lowering, "that would be nice. It feels like ages since I held you, or kissed you."

"Uh-huh." Jessica was suddenly overwhelmed by an urge to burst into tears. But she fought them back. She wasn't a clingy, dependent ninny like Sue. She would show Jeremy that she could be strong and brave and help him get through this, not make it harder. "Did I tell you about cheerleading practice yesterday?" she asked.

Jeremy chuckled. "No. How did it go? I can't wait to see you in that cute uniform."

In her room Jessica smiled. "It went OK. We've been working on a new routine. It won't be too long until it's homecoming."

"That'll be fun. Listen, I should get off soon—this is long distance. I don't want to run up my bill too much. But I promise that I'll be home before too long, and definitely before the Halloween party. I'll bring home matching costumes for us."

"That would be great," Jessica said, feeling more enthusiastic. "I'm a size six. And I'll tell everyone at school about the party."

"Good. OK, let me go now. I'll talk to you soon. I love you, Jessica."

"I love you too. I miss you."

"Whoa. That sundae never had a chance," Amy observed, watching as Jessica scraped up the last bit of hot-fudge sauce from her dish. It was Wednesday after school, and the two girls had gotten together to work on Amy's mood piece about Sweet Valley for the video club.

"I'm drowning my sorrow in ice cream," Jessica said sadly, wiping her lips with a napkin.

"What's the problem now?"

"Jeremy called last night, and it's going to be a while longer before he comes home."

Amy frowned. "That's like the third time he's been delayed."

"Yeah. It's because one of the other researchers had to leave early. Jeremy has to finish up his project."

"That's too bad."

"Mmm. Oh, but here's some fun news." Perking up a little, Jessica told Amy all about the big Halloween party at Project Nature's cabin. "That's when Jeremy and I are going to officially appear in public as a couple," she finished proudly.

"That sounds like a lot of fun," Amy said, her face brightening. "We can start spreading the word. It'll be the first party anyone's had so far this year."

"I know. Now tell me what you want me to do in this video thing of yours."

"You know that old pier at the very end of the beach? I want to film you standing there, wearing sunglasses and a scarf over your head, looking beautiful and sad and mysterious. It's cloudy today, so I think I can get some really interesting effects."

"Hmmm." Jessica pretended to think about it seriously. "Beautiful and sad and mysterious. I think I can do that." She gave Amy a mischievous smile.

Across the table from her, Amy cracked up. "Good. I knew I could count on you. Let's get going."

They paid their bill and went out to the black Jeep Jessica shared with Elizabeth. After they swung in and fastened their seat belts, Amy asked, "So what happened to boarding school? You had your interview almost two weeks ago, right?"

"Yes," Jessica said, wheeling the Jeep toward the beach. "Just yesterday morning Dad told me they had actually accepted me. But they haven't been throwing it in my face too much lately. I mean, they still don't want me to see Jeremy, but I'm trying to be cool around the house, you know, trying not to get them all riled up again. I still get little lectures every couple of days." She shook her head. "Can't they remember what it's like to be in love? Anyway, the weird thing is, Sue actually asked my parents not to do anything just yet. She insists that she's fine and everything's OK, and she doesn't miss Jeremy anymore, and that it's all going to work out for the best."

"That *is* weird."

"I can't figure it out. Why on earth would she want me around, when she's the last person I feel like seeing? She's really getting on my nerves. I'm just so tired of her always being there. Whenever I walk in the door, wham, there's Sue. The other day I came home, and she and Elizabeth were in the living room, sorting out all the wedding presents. I guess they all need to be sent back or something."

"Uh-huh. OK, turn here. You have to feel sorry for her—it must be so embarrassing, having to return everything. I mean, what is she going to say? 'Thanks anyway, false alarm'?"

Jessica grimaced and pulled into the parking lot opposite the old pier. "I know it's hard on her, and I'm sorry. It's been hard on everyone. But she's just always there, like she's taken over the house. She always gets the mail first. She almost always leaps on the phone first. Now she's started making dinner every night. Of course, that makes me look even worse," Jessica said sourly. "So I'm trying to be on my extra-best behavior."

"It's like there are two good twins, and then Jessica," Amy joked, leading Jessica out on the pier.

"Here, put these on." She handed Jessica a pair of old-fashioned sunglasses. "And this."

Jessica tied the gauzy scarf around her head, the way Grace Kelly had done in some old movie.

"OK, now stand at the end of the pier, kind of leaning on the rail," Amy directed her. "Look, Sue's probably just trying to be useful around the house. She knows she's stayed a really long time, and she just wants to help out and stay out of everyone's way. Now look away, out toward the water."

Amy quickly adjusted her video camera and took some experimental shots, trying to compensate for the cloudy afternoon.

"Yeah, I guess," Jessica groused. "But I just want her out of there!"

"Perfect! Keep that sullen expression," Amy cried.

I loooove this class, Elizabeth thought, watching Mr. Barton explain a graph equation. It was Friday after lunch, and Elizabeth was happily taking notes in her Go Math class. *Looove it. Love it. Just us girls getting stuff done, no asinine and immature boys, no spitballs, no belching, no stupid tricks. No loud male voices screaming out the answers. No hyperactive male feet tapping loudly on the floor, thumping against my desk. I love it.*

"Good, Molly," Mr. Barton was saying enthusiastically. "That's correct. And I'd like to compliment you on how much your performance has improved in the last couple of weeks. Well done."

At her desk Molly flushed, a pleased expression on her face.

Elizabeth shot her a thumbs-up. Molly smiled.

In fact, Elizabeth mused, almost every girl she had talked to who was in the Go Math classes had reported some increase in her grade. Elizabeth herself had usually done very well in math, but she realized that she had often waited until she got home to ask one of her parents about a problem she hadn't understood, rather than try to get an answer in school. With the boys in class, it was usually more of a struggle to get the teacher's attention. And then, of course, she thought with a mental sigh, the boys almost always teased someone who said they didn't understand. At any rate, her own math grades had risen from a high B+ to a solid A.

In her next installment of her Go Math series of articles, she was going to talk about some of the social differences between males and females, and point out how these differences could change the whole atmosphere of a class—often with detrimental results for the girls.

Mr. Barton asked for an answer, and Elizabeth raised her hand. "Yes, Elizabeth?"

"Y equals X minus forty-five?"

Mr. Barton smiled. "Correct. OK, now, today we're going to move on to a new concept in chapter three. Everyone turn to page fifty-four, and remember, if you have any questions, don't hesitate to ask."

Next to her, Enid turned and grinned at Elizabeth. "I had no idea I liked math!" she whispered.

Elizabeth nodded. English and languages had always been her favorite classes. She'd always had to put forth extra effort to do well in math. But she felt different about it now.

Elizabeth bit her lip. Math wasn't the only thing she felt different about. What in the world was she going to do about Todd? He looked like a used-car salesman. Not only that, but he really was acting differently as well—more insensitive or something. As though his haircut had affected his brain. She sat up straighter, a determined expression on her face. How shallow could she be? Todd was still the same person. She was simply going to have to forget about his appearance and concentrate on the person within—the person she had always loved.

But it was going to be tough.

For lunch Sue microwaved a vegetarian burrito, then took it out by the pool. It was nice to sit in the shade of the umbrella and eat, and read her magazine, and drink her lemonade. On the whole, things were OK. It had been a rough summer, but the end was in sight, and she knew she was going to make it. All she had to do was get through the next couple of weeks, and then everything would be all right. Just a couple more weeks.

For a while Sue lay in the sun, feeling the southern-California heat seep into her bones. She checked her watch. Still pretty early. When the cordless phone rang, she opened one eye lazily, then reached over to answer it.

"Hello? Oh, hey." Sue's face creased in a smile. "I'm doing fine—just catching some rays. Silly—it's only been two days. What are you doing, calling me now?"

The voice on the other end of the line said something, and Sue laughed. "No, no. Things are OK. Very quiet. . . . Yeah, no, I think I put an end to that. No one's said anything about it. . . . Oh, they're fine. Uh-huh. Yeah, she's fine. Please. You're kidding, right?"

For a while Sue just listened, laughing at jokes and nodding her head. She stretched out on the lounger and closed her eyes, enjoying the feeling of solitude. "No, you don't have to worry about that. I think once was enough . . . yeah, I definitely don't want to have my stomach pumped again. It was a total drag. I felt like a truck had rolled over me. Uh-huh. Yeah, you better go. Well, when will I see you again? OK. At our usual place? OK. Yeah, I understand. Quit worrying. Everything's fine. Uh-huh. OK, talk to you later. And I'll see you soon. Yeah, me too. 'Bye."

Sue clicked the off button and set the phone down on the pavement. She adjusted the straps of her bathing suit and peered down to see how her tan lines were progressing. Hmm. Might be time for some sunscreen. It was almost autumn, but the sun was still pretty strong, and she didn't want to get all red and itchy. She got up and headed inside to find some SPF 8.

"Hi."

"Hi." A week later on Saturday night, Lila stood in her doorway, looking at Robby. "I'm glad you came over," she managed to get out.

A look of relief washed over his face, and he smiled. His blue eyes creased at the edges, and he reached out to touch Lila's hand.

"I'm glad you asked me to," he said. "I've really missed you."

"Oh, Robby," Lila cried, throwing her arms around him. "I've missed you so much!"

For the next few minutes neither of them spoke as they hugged each other tight. Robby tangled his hands in Lila's long hair and held her as if she were water and he were dying of thirst. Lila snuggled as close to him as she could and locked her hands around his waist, enjoying the feel of his warmth and strength.

Finally she pulled away, laughing a little. "Maybe we better go inside, before the neighbors object."

"Good idea." Smiling, Robby followed Lila into Fowler Crest and down the hall. On their way past the den, he stopped in the open doorway to wave hello to Mr. and Mrs. Fowler.

"Robby," George Fowler said jovially. "Good to see you again."

"Honey, I think there's some chocolate mousse in the fridge if you two want a snack," Lila's mother said.

"Thanks, Mom. Maybe later." Taking Robby's hand, Lila led him downstairs to the rec room that opened up to the pool patio. There she put on some soft music, dimmed the lights, and sank down on one of the overstuffed couches.

"Come here," she said, patting the couch beside her. "We have a lot of lost time to make up for."

"Twist my arm," Robby said, sitting beside her and bending his head down to hers.

Much later they lay sprawled on the couch, lazily

watching a comedy show on TV. One lamp illumi-
nated the room.

"It's a good thing those stairs are there," Robby
said softly, stroking Lila's hair. "We can hear anyone
coming."

"Mmm." Lila smiled up at him, then took another
handful of popcorn. "Robby, let's agree that we won't
ever be apart like that again. These last few weeks
have been so awful. Let's promise never to be like
that again."

"Sounds good to me," Robby murmured. "Being
without you, not knowing when I would see you or
talk to you again, was murder. I could hardly sleep at
night."

"Me neither. Oh, you know what? Have you heard
the latest in the Jeremy-Jessica saga?"

Robby grinned. "Catch me up on all the hot gossip. I've been totally out of it lately." He sat up and
ate some popcorn.

"Well, of course you heard about Sue's whole suicide thing."

Robby frowned. "Yeah—that was awful. Is she
doing better now?"

"Uh-huh. So that blows over, and then Jessica
comes and says that Jeremy will be back for
Halloween, and there's a huge party at Project
Nature's cabin. So everyone's planning to go." She
turned bright eyes to him. "What should we go as?
Should we coordinate our costumes?"

Robby cuddled her closer. "I don't know. If I went
as a love slave, what would *you* wear?" He nuzzled
her neck.

"Robby!" Lila shrieked, laughing. "You're so bad."

Robby kissed her neck, lingering on the soft skin there. Slowly he lifted his head, and Lila looked up to see him gazing at her seriously.

"What?" she asked.

"I have a confession to make."

Lila stared up into his eyes. *What could it be? Did he go out with someone else?* "Wh-what are you talking about?" she stammered.

Robby pulled away from her and sat back on the couch. Looking down at the floor, he nervously twisted his hands together.

"It's about that business course," he began.

"Robby—forget about it!" *Did we make up just to break up? Is he going to hold that against me forever?*

"No, Lila—it's not what you think. The thing is, well . . . I know I was pretty mad about it. But then, a couple days before the course started, I kind of thought about it. And I decided that it wouldn't hurt to go just once, see what it was like. And if I hated it, I wouldn't go back." Robby looked up, an earnest expression on his face. "So I went. And . . . it wasn't as bad as I thought it would be. The teacher was taking everything really slowly, and by the end of class I realized I was kind of interested in what she was talking about."

Lila sat frozen next to him, unable to think of what to say.

Robby looked embarrassed. "So I got the textbooks and went back. And, well, I've been going ever since. We had our first quiz yesterday, and I got a ninety-two." He gave Lila a sheepish smile. "I just, you know, hope you don't hate me. This whole past month, with us arguing and all . . . I mean, after I put up such a fuss about it, and yelled at you and everything . . ." Robby looked down at his hands. "I hope you forgive me."

For a moment Lila just sat there, staring at him. He had been taking the business course for a month and not saying a word! And they had broken up about it! Then a tremendous smile spread across her face, and her eyes lit up with happiness. Jumping up, she flung herself into his arms and said, "Oh, Robby! I love you!"

Laughing, Robby kissed her face, her hair, anything he could reach. "Really?" he asked happily. "You're not mad? I know I was stupid and stubborn. . . ."

"Don't be silly," Lila said. "I'm just really glad you're taking the course."

Robby nodded. "Yeah, I think it'll be a good thing. And you know what? While I was on campus, I saw a notice for a drawing class. So I showed them my portfolio and they took me. My dad's boss is helping with the tuition, and to pay him back, I'm going to do a formal portrait of his fox terrier, Muffin." Robby grinned.

"That's great! Good for you. Two college courses, and you thought you'd never go," Lila teased him gently.

Robby blushed. "Yeah, well, I figured since I was making the commute, I might as well make it worth my while. So I'm enjoying this drawing class. It's much harder than any art class I've ever taken—it's really making me stretch."

139

"That's terrific. I'm so proud of you. It's one of the things I love about you—you're a go-getter. I bet you're the best artist in that class." Lila stroked his thick black hair lovingly.

Robby shrugged modestly. "I do OK. At first it was really hard keeping my concentration. Because of the nudes and all. But now it's a lot easier for me." He took a handful of popcorn and munched it.

"Excuse me?" Lila looked at him blankly. "The *nudes*?"

Chapter 11

"It's a life-drawing class. That means we draw from life. So they hire these professional artists' models to pose for us. It really helps us study the definition of muscles and bone structure. But it was weird at first."

"Are they women?"

"Well, some of them are," Robby said nonchalantly.

"Robby, are you telling me that you draw naked women *live*?"

"Sure. Oh, but, sweetie—" he said, comprehension crossing his face. "You have nothing to worry about. They don't even seem like people. They're professionals. I can't even remember their faces. All I think about is the drawing. Like an object." He rubbed Lila's back comfortingly.

"I *bet* you don't remember their faces," Lila snapped accusingly. She stood up, anger and a sense of fear making her practically tremble.

Robby frowned. "Lila—there's nothing improper about it. The teacher is there, and the students never talk to the models or vice versa. We don't even know their names. They just do this for a job."

"Oh, right!" Lila spat. The thought of Robby sitting in a class looking at naked women just completely sent her over the edge. It was totally unacceptable. Completely and totally.

"Lila! You don't understand," Robby said, his handsome face darkening with anger. "All art schools have life-drawing classes. Leonardo da Vinci was a master of life drawing. There's nothing wrong with my taking that class!" He strode around the rec room, his hands stiffly at his sides.

"I think there is!" Lila cried. She had never felt so angry at anyone in her life, and it didn't help to know that part of it was caused by a sickening jealousy.

"Well, you think wrong!" Robby said. He stopped pacing and rubbed his hand through his hair, making it stand on end. "I've explained how it is—you're just going to have to accept it. Until then I have nothing further to say!"

"Fine! Then leave," Lila shouted, her fists clenched. "Come back when you quit that stupid class!"

"I guess that'll be never, then!" Robby shouted back. With one last, angry look at her he stormed up the stairs. The front door was too far away for Lila to hear it, but she knew he had probably slammed it on the way out. Then she sank down onto the couch and hid her face in her hands.

❖   ❖   ❖

"Ah," Elizabeth said, taking a sip of her orange juice. "There's nothing like going out to breakfast on a beautiful Sunday morning." She grinned across the table at Sue, who was taking a bite of her pecan waffles.

"Umm-hmm," Sue said, chewing happily. "I'm really glad you suggested this, Elizabeth. This place is great."

Elizabeth smiled at the older girl. "I wish I wasn't in school all day during the week. It was fun in the summer when we could go do things—go to the mall, to the beach."

Sue reached for the maple syrup and nodded. "Yeah, I miss you during the day. But I've been filling my time." She took another bite. "These waffles are so fabulous. I'm in heaven."

"It's good to see you eating again," Elizabeth said seriously. "You look much better than you did a week or so ago."

It was true. Just in the past couple of days Sue had seemed to bloom, to look almost the way she had during the summer. She wasn't so pale and wan, her eyes were brighter, and it was obvious that she was crying less and sleeping better. When they had discovered Sue after her suicide attempt, Elizabeth had been shaken to the very core. It was incomprehensible to her that anyone close to her own age could consider ending her life. Especially over some guy.

Frankly, Elizabeth didn't see what either Sue or Jessica saw in Jeremy. She could hardly think of him without shivering in disgust. It seemed so clear to her that he was just a user. If she forced herself to be objective, she admitted that he was good-looking. But there were more important qualities than that—like loyalty, honesty, and trust. *Oh, yeah, you've really been relishing those things about Todd lately,* her conscience scolded her. *Apparently being handsome is pretty high on your list, after all.* Elizabeth squirmed uncomfortably.

"Well, I feel better," Sue agreed. "I've been seeing that therapist almost every day, and she's really helped me sort out my feelings. I'm totally over Jeremy now. In fact, there's a guy at Project Nature in New York who I used to be friends with. When I go back, I might ask him out on a date."

"Really?" Elizabeth was surprised. She had been hoping for Sue to recover from the blow of Jeremy's desertion, but it still hadn't been all that long ago. For Sue to feel that she was completely over such an important relationship seemed strange to Elizabeth. Maybe Sue was in denial or something. But she looked really sincere.

"Yeah. And I've been looking forward to getting all of Mom's money, after all," Sue said cheerfully. Then she quickly looked more serious. "I mean, I want to start looking into what charity will most benefit from a large contribution. Stuff like that. Although I might treat myself to a little trip to Europe. You know, to help me continue to recover." She nodded decisively.

"Oh, uh-huh," Elizabeth said slowly, looking at Sue across the table. For some reason she suddenly felt as though she were meeting Sue for the first time. "Would it be safe to go to Europe in your condition?" she asked, watching Sue's face. Elizabeth had had a feeling of dread and awful anticipation ever since she had found out about Sue's rare blood disease before the wedding. Just the knowledge that Sue's body might be dying even as her spirit was valiantly trying to recover had practically kept Elizabeth up nights. Now she was wondering if she was the only person worried about it.

For a moment Sue looked confused. Then her face suddenly cleared, and she nodded, almost to herself. She paused, seeming to consider something, then said, "Elizabeth—I have a confession to make."

"I'm an idiot," Lila moaned, stirring her strawberry smoothie. She and Jessica had met at the Valley Mall for a little shopping. They were taking a break at Smootharama, in the food court.

"Maybe, but you don't want Robby in a class full of naked women." Jessica spooned up the last bit of her pineapple-orange smoothie. "I mean, come on. I can't believe he expects you to not be bothered by it. What do you think of these earrings?" She held one earring up to her ear and turned it toward Lila. "Too much?"

"Uh-uh. Shoulder-dusters are still in. And I *am* totally bothered by it," Lila said. "I can't pretend that I'm not. I hate it. The very idea of Robby looking at someone naked just makes me want to die. I almost threw up when he told me last night."

Jessica made a face and put the earrings back in their package. "Right. I mean, what if he falls in love with one of them? You would totally lose him," she pointed out. "Come on. Let's go to Kiki's. I want to look at their fall miniskirts."

Lila got up and gathered all her packages. "I might have totally lost him already, since I threw such a fit last night," she said mournfully. They headed down a mall corridor to their favorite boutique.

"You were standing up for yourself," Jessica defended her. She paused to look at some shoes in a window. "Hey, these are on sale. Let's go in."

"Yeah, but now I'm all alone." Lila picked up a pair of woven-leather platform shoes. "These are cute. And after all, he does have to draw male nudes as well."

Jessica slowly turned to face Lila. Her eyes were round, and there was a suspicious gleam in her eyes. "You know, Lila, maybe one day we should drive up to SVU and check out his class. Maybe if we see for ourselves how professional and aboveboard everything is, we'll feel better. What days does he have this class?"

Lila gave an exaggerated sigh. "Jessica, you couldn't be more transparent if you were made of mountain-stream water." She mimicked Jessica's pseudo-innocent expression. "'See how professional it all is.'"

Jessica blushed. "Can't blame a girl for trying."

Laughing, Lila led them out of the shoe store. "You're impossible, Jess."

"Hang on a minute, will you?" Jessica said. "I suddenly have an intense desire to talk to my beloved. After all, it's been two days. It's OK if I use your card one more time, right?"

Lila shrugged and rolled her eyes.

Jessica dropped her packages in front of a pay phone and fished in her wallet for the calling card. Then she punched in a series of numbers and waited to be connected to Costa Rica. Lila watched her with an expression of mingled amusement and pity.

"Yes, hello?" Jessica said. "I'm calling for Jeremy."

Standing a few feet away, Lila said softly, "I'm sorry, Jeremy isn't here right now. Can I take a message?"

Jessica frowned at her and gripped the phone tighter. "He isn't? Oh. Well, could you tell him that Jessica called? Ask him to call me tonight. Thanks. 'Bye."

"What a surprise. Jeremy isn't there," Lila said sarcastically.

"He's working really hard," Jessica muttered. She kicked her shopping bag gently in disappointment.

"Jessica," Lila said, taking her arm. "I'm going to say one thing, and you can get mad at me if you want. But remember when you wanted to stay out late with Sam and didn't want your parents to know? When his folks were out of town?"

Jessica nodded cautiously.

"And Prince Albert got out, and your mom called you at my house to see if you had him?" Prince Albert was the Wakefields' golden retriever.

Jessica nodded again.

"And I said, 'Oh gosh, Mrs. Wakefield, Jessica's in the bathroom. I'll have her call you as soon as she gets out.' Then I called you at Sam's, and you called your mom back and said, 'I was washing my hair. What's up?'"

Frowning, Jessica demanded, "What's your point?"

Lila groaned and slapped her hand against her forehead. "Never mind. Don't worry about it. Forget I ever brought it up. There are none so blind as those who will not see." Turning away, she headed toward Kiki's with all her packages.

"Wait a minute, Lila," Jessica said, hurrying to catch up with her. "What did you mean? What are you implying?" *Geez, first Elizabeth, now Lila. Why does everyone want to rain on my parade?* Her mouth tight, Jessica followed Lila through the mall corridor, refusing to admit for even one minute that her old fears, her old premonitions about Jeremy, were stuck in her throat, right near the surface. And they were choking her.

"A confession?" Elizabeth asked. She pushed her plate away from her. *You're not really Sue Gibbons? You didn't really try to kill yourself? You and Jeremy are secretly married?* Elizabeth was surprised by the force of her reaction. Why on earth would she imagine those things?

"Yeah," Sue said. She looked down at her plate, embarrassed. "It's about my—the blood disease. The one that my mom died of, and that I said I had, too. . . ."

Elizabeth waited patiently.

"Well, I don't really have it," Sue blurted. "I never did. It's true that my mom died of it—but I made up the story about inheriting it." Her eyes darted back and forth, past Elizabeth's head. Her hands were rhythmically shredding her paper napkin. When she

148

spoke again, her voice was quiet. "It's just that, I could see what was happening between Jessica and Jeremy. I could see that I might lose him. And I just—couldn't bear the thought of it somehow. I just wanted to have him, no matter what. So I made up my illness, to try to make him stay with me. And for a little while it worked," she finished in a whisper.

Stunned. This feeling is stunned. Elizabeth sat as though glued to her chair, unable to think of anything to say. So many emotions were rushing through her: anger, relief, sadness, regret.

"I'll understand if you can't forgive me," Sue said, looking very sincere. "Now I see what a horrible thing it was to do. I've been so ashamed about it— dreading someone finding out the truth. You must think I'm a terrible person—so pathetic. I don't know what came over me. But it was totally wrong of me. And I'm so sorry. I'm so sorry, Elizabeth." Sue sat there, the picture of shame and dejection.

For a moment Elizabeth had no idea what to do. She thought of all the times she had comforted Sue—all the times she had commiserated with her about the final irony of having a fatal disease. All those times had been fake, all that emotion wasted. And yet Sue's explanation of her behavior did make a sort of bizarre sense. If Elizabeth were in that position, could she honestly say she wouldn't resort to subterfuge? She wasn't sure. So she really had to give Sue the benefit of the doubt.

"Well, Sue, I'm glad to hear it. I know I should be mad, but I've been so worried about your becoming deathly ill that I'm really relieved that it was a false alarm. I forgive you—I think I understand what made you say such a thing. I just want you to be healthy and happy."

Sue raised her head and gazed tremulously into Elizabeth's eyes. "Thanks, Liz. You don't know how much that means to me. I feel so much better, now that I've confessed. What a load off my mind." She gave Elizabeth a grateful smile.

"I feel better too. So let's just forget it ever happened."

Reaching across the table, Sue shook Elizabeth's hand. "It's a deal."

Elizabeth smiled at her, then finished the rest of her orange juice. She *was* relieved that Sue wasn't ill, but part of her was also troubled. It was such a huge thing to lie about. She never would have believed Sue capable of it. Elizabeth had been so upset, so heartbroken to hear about Sue's being sick, and all along it had just been a lie. . . . Had Sue lied about anything else?

Chapter 12

Winston sat in the barber's chair at Rigoberto's, silently regarding his reflection in the mirror. It was Tuesday afternoon after school. He had heard that this was Rigoberto's day off and had come in the hopes of having the new stylist, Tony, attempt to fix the series of hatchet jobs that his hair had already endured.

However, just as he had been sitting down in Tony's chair, comfortably settling in with an ancient copy of *Field and Stream*, Rigoberto had unexpectedly shown up.

"William!" he had cried happily. "What luck! I just stop in on my day off—and look. Here you are. Wait—you're my special customer. Tony—step aside. No one touches William's hair but me."

With that he had thrown off his jacket and donned his white barber coat. While Winston had sunk lower and lower in his chair, practically writhing with dread and disappointment, Rigoberto had stood over him, making aggressive snipping noises with his small scissors.

Now, fifteen minutes later, Winston knew what he would look like when he was sixty years old. He would look like his grandfather. He would be bald.

He sat there calmly, mustering up the strength to step down from the chair, pay his bill, and somehow make it home. At this point it no longer seemed to matter whether anyone saw him or not. If anyone asked, he could mumble something about being in a really cutting-edge band. That would shut them up.

"It's going to be a fabulous party," Jessica said as she dumped her books onto the desk next to Amy's.

The video club was holding a screening of all their first-project videos, and Jessica had shown up to see Amy's, as she had promised.

"Are you still talking about the Halloween party?" Dana Larson asked.

Jessica nodded excitedly. "Jeremy says that everyone at Sweet Valley High is invited. I just wish I could have helped with the planning. But Jeremy says it's all in the hands of the people who work there." She frowned. "It's a shame I can't give it the spectacular Jessica Wakefield touch, though. I hope they know what they're doing. Anyway, I can't wait to see what kind of costume he brings back for me. Do you guys have your costumes yet?"

Dana laughed. "It's not even the middle of October yet, Jessica. I think we have a little time to think about it."

"Well, if you want a really fantastic costume, you better start getting it together," Jessica advised. "I mean, this is going to be a totally hot party. Tons of older people will be there, not just teenagers. Maybe we should even have a costume contest."

"That's a fun idea," Amy agreed. "Dana, is your band going to play at the party?" Dana was the lead singer for The Droids, a popular rock band at school.

Dana shrugged. "We haven't been asked, but we don't have another gig for that night."

"I'll arrange it," Jessica said magnanimously. "Just let me ask Jeremy."

Just then the adviser for the video club, Mr. Sims, came in and began to look over the list of videos that had been turned in.

"OK, now . . . let's see. Why don't we show Amy's first?" he asked, looking up and smiling at Amy. "Would you care to tell us a little bit about it, Amy?"

Amy nodded. "I wanted to show the moody side of Sweet Valley. Everyone thinks of southern California as being really modern—all sunshine and surfers and pink stucco houses. I wanted to explore a darker, richer, less perfect side of our town." She turned to nod crisply at Scott Trost, who started the VCR at the front of the class.

Amy's movie was only about five minutes long, but Jessica enjoyed it. It was in black and white, and Amy had filmed some of the oldest buildings in the area. Some buildings looked very Spanish, and Amy had shot them so that they seemed even older and more romantic. There were other shots of lonely, windswept beaches, dark alleys lined with bamboo, and ancient oak trees overgrown with Spanish moss. It made Sweet Valley look completely different, really accenting its culture and history. The one scene with Jessica in it came out well and had a moody, wistful feeling.

"Wow!" Sandy Bacon started clapping as soon as the film was over. "That was great, Amy! I had no idea our little hometown could look so compelling!"

The other people in class agreed, and complimented Amy on the successful use of various lenses and filters, none of which Jessica understood.

"Now, who's next?" The teacher glanced at the list. "Is Winston here? I'd like to see his video."

There were a few murmured snickers in class, and someone muttered, "He's at the Telly Savalas look-alike contest." More laughter.

Jessica couldn't help grinning.

"Actually, Mr. Sims," Amy said, "Winston asked me to run his movie, although he couldn't be here. He's, uh—busy this afternoon."

More muffled snickers.

"Very well," the teacher said. "Roll 'em!"

Amy started Winston's cassette in the VCR, then came back to sit by Jessica.

"This is the one about the most romantic places in Sweet Valley," Amy whispered.

The movie started with a close-up of a road sign pointing to Miller's Point. Everyone in class whistled and hooted. Miller's Point was the best-known make-out spot in town.

But the movie took on a dreamy, sweet quality as the screen showed colorful, softly focused views of the rose garden at the Sweet Valley Botanical Garden, and a quaint bench hidden behind some flowering vine.

"I can almost smell the flowers," Amy whispered, and Jessica nodded. She would have to take note of these spots. Later she could bring Jeremy to all of them.

Then the scene segued into a shot of the back corner booth at the Dairi Burger, and everyone laughed. The mood changed again when a shadowy, private alcove at the museum came into view.

"Whoa—I didn't even know about that one," Scott said, and a couple of people laughed. "Is that right off the main stairs?"

Then the scene changed again, and it was a cloudy day at the beach. Hardly any people were around, and it looked quiet and peaceful. The camera panned down the beach. Several couples were walking along, holding hands. It was Moon Beach, about twenty minutes north of the city—the beach where Jessica had called Sue and Jeremy's wedding to a halt.

Suddenly Jessica sat frozen in her chair, her eyes glued to the video screen. A man was walking alongside the cement beach wall, a man with tangled, sunstreaked blond hair and an easy tiger's walk. A man who looked exactly like Jeremy.

Without taking her eyes from the screen, Jessica whispered to Amy, "When did Winston film this?"

Amy thought for a moment. "Well, it was cloudy," she whispered back. "So it must have been the same day I filmed you at the beach in Sweet Valley. It hasn't been cloudy since then. About two weeks ago, I guess. Why?"

"No reason."

It's ridiculous, impossible. Stop doing this to your-self, Jess. She smiled to herself, thinking about what a romantic idiot she was. She was so in love with Jeremy that she saw him everywhere. He was on her mind so much that every man looked like him.

But she couldn't help the little frown lines that appeared between her brows as she watched the screen. The man in Winston's video did look amazingly like Jeremy. Of course, he was a long way away, and very small on-screen. But he moved like Jeremy, walked like him, shook back his hair like him. It was really weird.

Just then a dark-haired woman dressed in shorts and a white fisherman sweater stood up and walked over to meet the man. He put his arms around her and they kissed deeply.

The students in the class hooted and clapped their hands.

"Way to go, man!" Bill Chase slapped an imaginary high five.

Far away on the lonely, cloudy beach, the couple continued to hug and kiss, then started to walk toward the camera, their hands interlocked. They were so small that their features were indistinct. But it was clear that they were talking seriously about something, and that they were all wrapped up in each other. Then the golden-headed man looked up and happened to see Winston filming them, hundreds of feet away. He said something to the woman, and the two turned and headed down the beach in the other direction.

"Privacy, please!" Amy said with a laugh.

But Jessica didn't smile. Of course it was just a freaky coincidence. Of course they were complete strangers whom she'd never seen before. Of course Sue was at the Wakefields' house during the day, and of course Jeremy was thousands of miles away in Costa Rica, doing his field research. Those things were all true, were all facts.

But if Jessica hadn't known that they were true, hadn't known that that was how things were beyond a shadow of a doubt, she would have sworn that man was Jeremy, and that woman was Sue, and they were kissing and holding each other as though they hadn't been together in a long time and were vowing never to be apart again.

Jess, get a grip. You're just being crazy because you haven't seen him in so long. Hang on—it's just a few more days. Just get it together.

"So, Elizabeth, I finished reading this week's article on the Go Math program," Mr. Collins said. "You turned it in a day early." He looked meaningfully around at the other newspaper staff members. Tina Ayala, Olivia Davidson, and Cheryl Thomas all laughed.

"That's our Elizabeth," Andy Jenkins said playfully.

"It's just that I've gotten so caught up in the whole girls-only curriculum," Elizabeth said. "In my latest article I'm suggesting that they have segregated-sex science classes as well next semester. Do you know that virtually every single girl in my class has improved her overall math score?"

"Yeah, but you guys are two lessons behind us in the textbook," Andy said patiently.

"I bet by the end of the year we'll have done exactly as much work as you, and done it better," Elizabeth said vehemently. "We're taking our time now because so many girls have needed to review the basics. We were never encouraged to ask questions in class before. But we're progressing at a faster rate now. It won't be long before we catch up."

"The statistics that you've attached to your article certainly help support your case," Mr. Collins said. "How did your interviews with grade-school students turn out?"

Elizabeth smiled. "They were fine. Almost all the girls in the segregated math class report that they're enjoying math more than they did when there were boys in the class. They say it's easier to concentrate, and it's nice not to have, quote, stinky guys, unquote, cutting up all the time and making fun of them. However"—Elizabeth consulted her notes—"the boys are not as enthusiastic. They miss the girls. One boy said he liked looking at girls during class. Another boy said he thought having girls in class made the class 'nicer and quieter.' And one fifth-grade male chauvinist piglet said he wanted girls in class because it made his math skills look better." Elizabeth stopped and made an exasperated face. "Please. I feel sorry for his girlfriend when he grows up."

Tina laughed. "It's hard to believe that kids are so different, male and female, even at such a young age."

"Let's face it—it's hard to believe that the human race has managed to propagate, given what we

158

women are forced to work with," Elizabeth said jokingly.

"Hey!" Andy Jenkins looked to Mr. Collins for support. "Are you going to let them talk this way about us?"

Mr. Collins laughed and held up his hands. "It's a free country," he reminded Andy. "Not only that, but a smart man knows when to retreat."

Elizabeth and Olivia gave each other high fives. "You know it," Elizabeth said.

"There's one exciting announcement I have to make," Mr. Collins said, tapping his pencil against his notebook. "Elizabeth, your series of articles on the Go Math program has been picked up by the local news service. They'll start appearing in the *Sweet Valley News* next month. Congratulations."

While Elizabeth sat in her chair in shock, her hand to her throat, Mr. Collins continued.

"That's what happens to strongly written, well-researched, timely stories of general interest. So let that be a lesson to all of you."

Olivia and Tina both reached over and slapped high fives with Elizabeth again.

Soon the *Oracle* staff meeting was adjourned, and, still laughing and joking, the students filed out into the hall. Elizabeth walked out with Olivia, talking about possible costumes for the Halloween party at the end of the month.

"Hey, Liz." Todd was waiting for her outside the staff room. "Basketball practice let out early. I was hoping to catch you." He smiled and leaned over to brush a kiss against her cheek.

"Oh, hi, Todd," Elizabeth said, feeling the familiar wash of guilt that came over her lately every time she saw Todd. "That was sweet of you. Have a good practice?"

Awkwardly she tried to make conversation, telling Todd as they walked down the hall about her articles being picked up by the local newspaper, but Elizabeth was burningly aware of Olivia's sympathetic smile. *Oh, stop it,* she told herself firmly. *You're being awful. This is Todd. Quit being so mean to him.* She forced herself to look up at Todd and smile at him.

He smiled back tentatively. Elizabeth knew that the way she had been treating him had had a bad effect on their relationship, but she felt powerless to stop it. It wasn't just the mustache, she thought. Somehow his attitude had changed along with his appearance. For example, she argued silently, he had started calling her "babe" right after he got his new haircut. He never called her "babe" before. She hated being called "babe." But he was doing it.

They trooped down the front steps of the school, Todd, Elizabeth, and Olivia. It was getting darker earlier now, though the days were still warm and sunny. And another thing. He had been driving a little faster lately, taking turns a tiny bit more recklessly. It was his hair. It was making him do it. Suddenly he was a new person, a stranger, and though he had a lot of Todd's good qualities, still, he was different. It would take her a while to get used to him. If she ever would. If she even wanted to.

"Elizabeth, should I take that as a no?"

Elizabeth, startled, glanced up and saw Todd gazing at her with a clearly annoyed expression.

"I'm sorry—what did you say?" she asked.

"I said, 'Do you want a ride home?'" he said angrily. "But since I've asked twice and you've ignored me, I guess you don't. So I'll see you later." Without looking back at her, he spun on his heel and stormed down the steps to where his car was parked. "Todd, wait! I didn't mean—" Elizabeth broke off, watching Todd's retreating back. She sighed.

"Need a ride home?" Olivia asked softly.

"Yes, please," Elizabeth answered. She gave Olivia a rueful look. "Could we stop on the way and get me a new brain while we're at it?"

Chapter 13

"Out of my way!" Jessica screeched, tearing around the corner and leaping into the bathroom she shared with Elizabeth.

Elizabeth was flung back against the wall, her stack of folded laundry almost tumbling out of her hands. After dumping the clothes onto her bed, she poked her head into the bathroom.

"What is with *you* tonight?" she demanded. "I mean, I know it's Friday, but is it a full moon?"

"Tonight, tonight," Jessica warbled as she made a kissy-face so that she could apply blush to the fullest part of her cheeks. "I'll be with him tonight," she sang.

Elizabeth's eyes widened. "You're kidding. Jeremy's finally back in town?" She frowned. Somehow she was hoping that he would simply never come back. She'd rather help Jessica get over that than, well, get over whatever he might do to her. Dump her in person or whatever.

Jessica nodded happily. "Don't tell Mom and Dad," she whispered loudly, digging in the makeup drawer for some mascara. "But I'm meeting him tonight in back of the Beach Cafe." She wheeled to face Elizabeth, her eyes aglow with excitement. "Can you believe it? He's been gone almost two whole months. The Halloween party is the day after tomorrow." She burst into song again. "My boyfriend's back, and there's gonna be trouble," she sang through her giggles. Then her face sobered, and she began to curl her eyelashes. "Actually, I hope there won't be any trouble. Although we're going to announce our engagement officially at the party, I hope that everyone will be cool about it. Jeremy and I have talked about it, and we've decided that we're just going to take it easy and play it by ear." Jessica regarded her reflection critically, then searched for the right shade of lipstick. "I mean, we both know we're going to be together forever, so we don't really have to make a huge statement now." Her words became garbled as she pursed her mouth to outline her lips. "After aw, Sue wi' be gone 'oon." She finished her mouth, then leaned over to fluff up her hair. "And I still have to live at home. So we might as well try to avoid any huge blowups for a while. I don't want Milford Military Academy brought up again. Besides, if I had to go through one scene after the other until I'm eighteen, I would just end up with ulcers."

"Hmm." Elizabeth crossed her arms and watched Jessica put the finishing touches on her makeup.

Suddenly she felt grumpy and nervous, and it was all because that rat Jeremy was back in town.

"Tonight, tonight," Jessica sang, "won't be just any night. . . ."

"Well, you look fabulous," Elizabeth said, feeling more than a little trepidation. "I hope everything goes all right," she added insincerely.

Jessica caught her eye in the mirror. "What are you doing tonight? Where's the Todd-ster?"

Elizabeth made a face. "We're practically hardly even dating anymore," she admitted. "We're still supposed to go to the Halloween party together, but I haven't seen him outside of school in almost a week." She shrugged her shoulders. "Sue and I are going to go hit a movie. So whatever you do, don't go to the Valley Mall. If Jeremy and Sue run into each other, I do *not* want to be there."

Jessica giggled. "Don't worry. We'll probably just walk on the beach beneath the stars for a while, then maybe go to Miller's Point." She winked at Elizabeth.

Her sister came to stand behind her in the mirror and put a hand on Jessica's shoulder. "Jessica, please be careful," she said in a serious tone. "I couldn't bear it if you got hurt. OK?"

Jessica cheerfully patted her hand. "You worry too much."

"So what movie should we go see?" Elizabeth asked, spreading out the newspaper on Sue's bed.

"Hmm, I don't know. How about that foreign film?" Sue pointed to a movie ad.

"I usually like foreign movies, but I heard that

one was pretty weird," Elizabeth said doubtfully. "But there's a new movie out by Rufus Barry. He's hysterical. I love that British humor."

"Yeah, maybe we should see that."

Sue leaned over the paper and continued to peruse the ads. Elizabeth took a moment to examine Sue surreptitiously. Her face was calm and relaxed, her hair looked shiny and brushed, and her clothes were fitting her better. On the whole, the older girl looked better than she had since the wedding— happy and healthy and excited. Just like the old Sue. But now Jeremy was back in town.

Sue sat back, a cheerful expression on her face. "Yeah, let's see *Happiness Is a Warm Scone*," she said. "It'll be good to laugh for a couple of hours."

"OK, sounds good," Elizabeth agreed. She stood up and brushed off the knees of her black leggings. "We should probably leave in about half an hour."

"Okeydokey," Sue said, sitting back and crossing her legs. "Oh, Elizabeth—I wanted to ask you. What are you going to wear to the Project Nature Halloween party? Are you and Todd going to coordinate?"

Elizabeth was surprised, though when she thought about it, she realized she probably shouldn't be. After all, Sue had been working for Project Nature—of course she would know about the party. And with her current all-tolerant attitude, she probably even knew, and accepted, the fact that it was going to be Jeremy and Jessica's big coming-out party.

"Yeah, we're supposed to go together," she said. "Although the way we've been getting along lately, it

165

would be a miracle if we made it through the whole party without wringing each other's neck. I'm just going to resurrect last year's costume of a black cat, and I don't even know what Todd is going to be."

"I think I'm going to be a witch," Sue said enthusiastically. "It should be pretty simple to put together a costume: black leggings, a black turtleneck, and I could buy a cheap cape and a pointy hat at that costume shop on the highway." Her brown eyes sparkled. "It's going to be a great party, with a live band and everything. I'm really looking forward to it."

"Um-hmm." Elizabeth nodded noncommittally. Her eye had just been caught by a faint shadow on Sue's neck. It was mostly hidden by the collar of Sue's shirt, but it looked like some kind of bruise. Elizabeth prayed that Sue hadn't tried to hurt herself again. She hoped that Sue's attitude was genuine, and not just a cover-up for some unfathomable desperation.

"And one more thing, Elizabeth," Sue said. "I want to go to the party to show everyone that I really don't have any hard feelings against Jeremy or Jessica. I feel like if I stay home that night, everyone will just be thinking 'Poor Sue' and feeling sorry for me. And I just couldn't bear that. Do you understand?"

"Yeah, I do," Elizabeth said slowly. "I would probably feel the same way. I just hope that you're strong enough to handle it."

Sue nodded decisively. "I really feel as though I am, Liz. I'm much better now and ready to look ahead. I'm ready to move on with my life—without

Jeremy." She smiled at Elizabeth, but Elizabeth wasn't sure if the smile reached Sue's eyes.

"Jeremy!" Jessica used every ounce of willpower not to run to Jeremy and throw her arms around him. But they were in a public place, and she was being Ms. Maturity.

At the sound of her voice Jeremy turned, and his tanned, handsome face lit up. "Jessica!" He strode quickly toward her, then swept her up in his arms and twirled her around. It was already dark out, and the lights from the porch of the Beach Cafe spilled onto the white sand, making it glisten and sparkle.

Jessica laughed happily, feeling whole again. The last two months had been practically the hardest two months of her entire life, but she had made it through. Now Jeremy was home again and in her arms, and all was right with the world.

He put her down gently and enfolded her in a powerful hug. Jessica held him close and looked up into his midnight-dark eyes. Her breath caught in her throat. *God, he is so good-looking.* At his intense gaze Jessica blushed and looked down, suddenly feeling unsure and shy. Then he tilted up her face gently and covered her lips with his own, and all her uncertainty was washed away in a tide of longing.

For long moments they kissed, unmindful of the public beach they were on. The cool darkness of the autumn night surrounded them, making Jessica feel safe and private. Eagerly she drank in Jeremy's kisses as though she had never kissed anyone before. His hands roamed through her long, loose blond hair, holding her mouth firmly against his.

Finally he pulled back, breaking their kiss. He was breathing harder, and his eyes glittered.

"You know, until this moment I didn't even realize how much I missed you," Jeremy said thickly.

Jessica leaned against him, relishing his familiar touch that she had gone without for so long. "Well, I realized how much *I* missed *you*," she said. She smiled up at him, happy tears glittering in her beautiful blue-green eyes.

Slowly they moved down the beach, away from the cafe's lights and deeper into the darkness of the night. Medium-sized waves crashed rhythmically on the shore, their peaks frothy, lace-edged caps in the moonlight.

For long minutes Jeremy and Jessica walked, holding hands, Jessica's head leaning on his shoulder. When they came across a wooden bench set back from the sand, Jeremy sank down onto it, pulling Jessica to sit beside him. There she snuggled against him, letting his body shield her from the cool autumn breezes. In silence they watched the waves as Jeremy stroked Jessica's hair and brushed kisses along her brow. When she raised her face to look at him, he claimed her mouth again and they kissed deeply.

"You almost make me lose my head," Jeremy whispered hoarsely.

"Almost?" Jessica asked teasingly, and was rewarded with a crooked smile.

"Yes. Almost. At least one of us can remember that you're underage," Jeremy told her, and she laughed.

"Oh, it's so good to have you home again." She sighed happily. "You wouldn't believe all the stuff that's been happening." In their phone conversations she had mentioned the boarding school, and Lila and Robby's almost-breakup, and the other various tensions and problems that had been going on while he was away—but now they could talk about them in more detail. She gave him the full, unvarnished account of Lila's finding out about Robby's drawing class and told it in an amusing, dramatic way to make him laugh.

"So I told her, 'Lila, just go over to his house and say that if he wants to draw naked girls, he can draw *you*.'" Jessica's laughter floated out into the fresh night air. "I thought she was going to have a heart attack. She threw part of her hot-dog bun at me, right there at the Dog House in the mall. I almost died laughing."

Jeremy laughed too. "You're bad," he teased her. "So is Lila going to do it?"

Jessica made a face. "Oh, right. I'm so sure. Please. No, I don't know what she's going to do, but I don't think it's going to be *that*."

"Rats. I'm sure Robby's disappointed. How's Elizabeth?"

Jessica told him all about Elizabeth's reaction to Todd's new look. "I mean, he never really did it for me anyway, but now he's total bow-wow city," she concluded.

"And what about Sue?" Jeremy asked lightly, casually. "No ill effects from her suicide attempt?"

Next to him, Jessica froze. *How does he know*

about that? She had deliberately not mentioned it in their phone conversations.

"What?" she stammered, stalling for time.

"Look, just because I love you and want to marry you doesn't mean I was glad when you told me about that. Is she OK now?" Jeremy snuggled closer to her and kissed her gently along the side of her ear, making her shiver.

"Jeremy, I never told you about it," Jessica said, feeling confused. "Although Sue's fine now," she added quickly.

Jeremy gave her a tolerant smile. "Sure you did, sweetie. A couple of weeks ago. You just mentioned it in passing, and I said, 'Oh, how is she?' and you said, 'Fine,' and then we dropped it. I didn't worry about it because you didn't sound worried. But I'm glad to hear she's OK now. So are you looking forward to the party?" he asked, changing the subject.

For a moment Jessica didn't answer, still trying to puzzle through the mystery of the conversation that she was sure hadn't happened. But Jeremy seemed so sure it *had*. . . . Was it possible that she had mentioned it just in passing and then forgotten about it? It was so hard to remember. She had really *thought* she hadn't, but sometimes when she'd talked to him, she'd been so emotional and upset and lonesome—who knew what she had said? She just couldn't remember. . . .

"Jessica, aren't you excited about the party?" Jeremy pressed.

"Oh, yeah, of course I am." Jessica tried to put her troubling thoughts out of her mind. "I've been looking forward to it for so long. It's going to be great. And we'll announce our engagement." She forced a smile. "How should we do it? Should we have the band stop and hand you the microphone?"

Jeremy laughed and rubbed his hand across his eyes. "Yeah, sounds good. We'll do something like that."

In the darkness Jessica felt a cool breeze wash over her heart. Jeremy was being so offhand about it—as though it didn't really matter. But the whole idea behind the party was that they would officially announce being a couple, being engaged. Hadn't he thought about it a million times, as she had? Didn't he have plans for them? Unwilling to press him for details, and to cover her confusion, she said, "Well, I can't wait to see what costume you brought for me."

Jeremy sat up. "I got them in Los Angeles, on my way back from Costa Rica. But it's going to be a secret until right before the party. I'll drop it off on Sunday afternoon."

Jessica loved surprises. "I bet it's fabulous," she said, the warmth returning to her voice. "I hope it fits."

"Don't worry," Jeremy said, bending down for another kiss. "I made sure it was a perfect size six."

"Do you think I need a jacket?" Sue asked, shoving her feet into a pair of loafers.

"Yeah, maybe a light one," Elizabeth called as she headed down to her own room to get ready. While she was brushing her hair in the bathroom, she heard the faint peal of the doorbell.

A few moments later her mother called, "Elizabeth! I'm sending Todd up."

Her face fell as she stared into the mirror. *Darn. A few more minutes and I would have been out of here.* Todd's footsteps started pounding up the stairs. Then he tapped gently at her bedroom door.

"Hi, Todd," Elizabeth said, opening her door. "Gee, I didn't know you were coming over. Sue and I are just about to go to a movie." She paused awkwardly, not wanting to invite him to come along.

"This'll just take a minute," Todd said gruffly, entering her room and shutting the door behind him. He was frowning and looked preoccupied. One hand nervously stroked the hated mustache.

"Uh, Todd, Mom likes me to keep the door open when you're visiting," Elizabeth said faintly, moving over to her door.

Todd put his arm out and stopped her. "Hold on. We need a few minutes' privacy."

Elizabeth stopped, her hands on her hips. "What's going on?"

Todd laughed sardonically. "Not much, apparently. I can remember when you never would have made plans on a Friday night without asking me first. But since you hardly even talk to me anymore, when would you have mentioned it?" He strode angrily into the room, his arms crossed over his chest.

"You're avoiding me, Elizabeth. You've been treating me like garbage for weeks. You won't kiss me anymore, you don't want to go out and do things—I'm sick of it. Why don't we just break up now and get it over with?"

Elizabeth was shocked. Somehow she had convinced herself that she could just ride out the whole mustache fiasco, and that soon Todd would come to his senses and get rid of it, and then things would quickly go back to normal.

"Break up?" she repeated stupidly. "We're supposed to go to the Halloween party together."

"Yeah? What are you going to dress as? A witch? 'Cause you sure have been being one lately." Todd glared at her angrily and jammed his backward baseball cap firmly down on his head.

A spark of anger started to rise in Elizabeth. "OK, I'll go as a witch if you dress as a complete idiot, which is what *you've* been lately."

"What?" Todd glared at her.

"No, make that not only a complete idiot," Elizabeth rushed on, her voice growing louder, "but a fashion *disaster* as well! Look at yourself! No wonder I don't want to go out with you! You look awful."

Todd simply stared at her, his mouth open. Slowly he turned and looked at himself in the mirror over her dresser, stooping a little so he could see his face.

"What's wrong with how I look?" he said finally, still gazing at her incredulously.

"It's that stupid *mustache*, Todd!" Elizabeth snapped. "Or that grotesque growth you call your mustache. It's awful, it's hideous. You look like you should be out stealing cars or something. I hate it!" Suddenly Elizabeth felt close to tears. Normally she was slow to anger, and she couldn't remember the last time she had said such mean things to anyone. But her feelings had been building up at a slow boil for almost two months, and now she felt as though she were on a roller coaster of emotion that she simply couldn't get off.

"It scratches me when I kiss you. You're always playing with it. Between that and the haircut, I don't know what's worse." Elizabeth stomped over to her bed and sat down hard. She crossed her arms and glared at the floor. *This is it. We're breaking up. I didn't think it would be like this.*

"My haircut, too?" Todd practically shouted. "Now what's the matter with my haircut? It's totally cool!"

"It's totally horrible," Elizabeth cried defiantly. "You look like a surfer geek. And you've been calling me 'babe'! I *hate* that!" Suddenly she was crying as the release of finally getting all these feelings off her chest rushed through her. She grabbed a tissue from the box by her bed and wept into it.

"All guys call their girls 'babe,'" Todd insisted. He stormed around the room in the circle, waving his arms. "So now it all comes out. You hate my mustache, you hate my haircut, you hate what I call you. Well, let me tell you something, Ms. Picky and Judgmental Wakefield: kids at school think my mustache is hot, this is a totally radical haircut, and maybe I just won't call you anything from now on. As in, I won't be calling you at all!"

He stood there, his face an angry mask, as he glared at her crying on her bed.

Tears running down her face, feeling like a fool, Elizabeth yelled, "News flash, Todd. The only people at school who like your lip growth are guys as dense as you are. All the girls have been teasing me about it nonstop. They feel *sorry* for me! And that might be a totally radical haircut, but it makes you look like you stuck your head in a pencil sharpener. And if you quit calling me, I guess I won't have to come up with excuses to not be seen with someone who looks like his name should be on a juvenile detention list!" With that she flung herself facedown on her bed and started sobbing harder.

Todd stood there for a moment, looking totally dumbfounded; then with a muttered snarl he yanked her door open and stomped down the stairs. "I'll let myself out!" he shouted.

"Robby! Someone here to see you," Mr. Goodman called over his shoulder, giving Lila an encouraging smile. "He'll be down in a second, dear," he told her.

"Thank you," Lila said awkwardly. It was unusual for her to be calling on a guy at his house; they almost always came to her place. But she knew that Robby wasn't likely to show up at her door anytime soon.

Robby came running down the stairs into the entrance hall, then stopped dead when he saw her. His face fell, and his eyes shuttered their feelings. Tightly, he said, "Lila. This is a surprise."

Lila took a deep breath. "That's me," she joked weakly. "Full of surprises." She looked at the floor, aware of his eyes on her. She had taken extra care with her appearance and was wearing black velour leggings and a cream crocheted sweater with a cream silk camisole underneath. Robby had once said he thought it looked sexy.

175

"What can I do for you?" Robby asked shortly.

Mr. Goodman stood there awkwardly, apparently not knowing what to do or say.

"Can we talk?" Lila asked softly.

Robby seemed to consider the idea for a moment. Then he shrugged. "I guess so. Come on up." He stood aside so she could precede him up the stairs to his room.

"Uh, Robby," Mr. Goodman said quickly. "How about if you take Lila back to the family room? I'll clear out of there, and you two can have it to yourselves." He bustled down the hall toward the back of their small cottage.

Lila met Robby's eyes, and almost unwillingly, they both smiled.

"Dad is nothing if not circumspect," Robby said primly, and Lila almost giggled.

In the family room Lila and Robby sat down stiffly apart from each other.

"Robby, I—"

"So what do—"

They both stopped awkwardly; then Robby motioned for Lila to go first.

"I was wrong," she said simply.

Across from her Robby's eyes widened, but he said nothing.

It had taken Lila days of practicing in front of the mirror to get those words out—she had never said them before. *Oh no, is he going to make me say that I'm sorry, too?*

"About the drawing class?"

"Yes, of course. What else is there?" Lila said, a trifle

impatiently. She was embarrassed about having to be wrong, and she wanted it over with as soon as possible.

"Oh, nothing," Robby said, hastily swallowing a grin. "Well, that's very big of you, Lila. I'm glad to hear that you've changed your mind."

"Yeah," Lila said softly, her toe making circles on the carpet.

Robby slid off his chair and knelt in front of Lila. He rested his elbows on her knees and took her face in his hands. Then slowly, deliberately, he pulled her head down so his mouth could reach hers. With a little sigh of relief, Lila kissed him deeply, letting her kisses say the things that were too difficult for her to get out. Minutes later they were close together on the couch, with Lila's knees across Robby's lap as he played with her hair.

"So we're back together again, huh?" he asked, his voice rough.

Lila nodded wordlessly, her brown eyes shining up into his blue ones.

"You know I would never fool around on you," he said gruffly. "I can sit there and draw those people, but you're the only person I really *see*, Lila. Do you know what I mean?"

Lila met his eyes shyly. She couldn't believe he was saying all the things she needed to hear so desperately. "I think so," she said in a small voice.

"Good." He leaned back against the couch and pulled her closer, running his hand up and down her back in a very comforting way. "Wait till you see the costume I made you," he whispered into her ear.

Chapter 14

"Is this a fabulous costume or what?" Jessica crowed, gently nudging Elizabeth out of the way of the bathroom mirror.

"Mmm," Elizabeth said, slowly painting her nose black in an upside-down triangle.

Jessica swirled around experimentally, watching her sheer sleeves billow. She was dressed as Princess Jasmine from the Aladdin movie. The costume Jeremy had brought her had a pale-green close-fitting midriff top with sheer, extremely full sleeves trimmed in gold. The harem-style pants, also trimmed in gold, were low-waisted and slim-hipped, then flared out into billowy legs that tapered to narrow ankles. Small slippers were on Jessica's feet, and a gold band with a huge fake pearl held her hair off her face.

"So you'll give me a ride, right? I don't want Jeremy to have to face Mom and Dad. Jeremy's going as Aladdin, of course," Jessica continued. "Maybe tonight . . ." She stopped suddenly.

"What?" Elizabeth asked.

"Oh, nothing," Jessica said. "It's just that he's been, well, I don't know. Kind of preoccupied. I mean, he's only been back two days, but I've hardly seen him. He keeps having all these other things to do." She made a face, then shook her head, as though determined to put it out of her mind. "He's probably just worried about the party. I'm not going to think about it. Tonight everything will be perfect between us." She swirled around again, then settled down to the serious business of making up her face. "I'm going to do lots of heavy black eyeliner," she informed her sister, "and I think I'll put a black beauty mark on my cheek." She squinted in the mirror, guessing what the effect would look like, then got started.

Carefully Elizabeth started painting black whiskers across her cheeks.

Jessica frowned at her in the mirror, examining the black-velvet cat costume. "Isn't that what you wore last year?"

"Uh-huh."

"Why didn't you get a new costume? Everyone's seen that one before."

"Oh, like I care," Elizabeth muttered, outlining her eyes to make them look more elongated.

Jessica stopped what she was doing. "What on earth is the matter with *you*?" she demanded.

Elizabeth sighed. "I don't mean to take it out on you, Jess. But Todd and I broke up, and I didn't have the energy to get another costume, and I don't even know if he's going to be at the party tonight, and on the whole I would really rather not go. I'd rather just stay home and hand out candy corn to trick-or-treaters."

Jessica patted her shoulder. "Frankly, Liz, the way Todd's been looking lately, you're better off without him. Now get with the program," she said firmly. "That's what parties are for: so you can scope out some new guy. You could get yourself an older man, like Jeremy."

Elizabeth looked at Jessica. "The *last* thing I want is a man like Jeremy," she said darkly.

But Jessica was in too good a mood to take offense. "Suit yourself," she said airily.

"Knock, knock," Sue's voice sang. She tapped on Elizabeth's door to the bathroom and poked her head around. "Could you guys give me some advice? Does my costume need any finishing touches?"

Elizabeth turned. Sue was dressed simply in black leggings and a black turtleneck, as she had planned, and she had a long, swirling cape, a pointy black witch's hat, and a long, bedraggled black wig on her head. She had put a light-green tint all over her face and shaded in dark circles under her eyes.

"Wow, you look great," Elizabeth exclaimed. "Very witchy."

"Good costume," Jessica agreed.

"Oh, Jessica, you look terrific," Sue reciprocated. "Just like a blond Princess Jasmine."

"I think you need some very dark-red lipstick," Elizabeth decided, examining Sue's face. "Then you'll be all set."

For a few minutes, Elizabeth thought, as the three girls crowded together in the bathroom, it was like old times—when Sue had first arrived, when Jessica and Elizabeth and Sue had hung out together, gallivanting all over Sweet Valley. It had been a lot of fun. Then Jeremy had arrived, and everything had changed—for the worse. Now, looking at her sister and Sue being carefully polite to each other, pretending that they didn't hate each other, Elizabeth felt a sharp sense of foreboding. With Jeremy gone for so long, things had felt a bit more normal. Now Jeremy was back, Jessica was headed for major trouble, and Sue suddenly seemed like a stranger full of secrets.

When Elizabeth pulled the black Jeep to a stop at Project Nature's cabin, the party was already jumping. The cabin was set in a nature preserve about half an hour from Sweet Valley, but the three girls had found it easily. A landscaped yard surrounded the cabin and faded gently into woods. Chinese lanterns were strung between trees, swaying in the mild autumn breeze.

"It's a good thing it's pretty warm tonight," Elizabeth told Jessica. "Considering your outfit."

"Even if it were freezing, I wouldn't wear a jacket," Jessica said gaily. She pranced ahead, looking for Jeremy, her gold spangles dancing as she moved.

"She's so full of life," Sue said admiringly, watching Jessica plunge into the crowd.

Glancing at her, Elizabeth tried to gauge Sue's reaction. "That's one word for it," she said dryly. "Why don't we get something to drink?" *I shouldn't have even come tonight. I don't want to see Todd, and I certainly don't want to see Jessica hanging all over that jerk. And I don't want to see Sue and Jessica pretend to be nice to each other. Maybe I should just shut my eyes now and feel my way back to the Jeep.*

They moved past the stage, where the band was belting out loud, raucous music. The name of the band was spray-painted on a banner: The Nontoxic Avengers. But Elizabeth thought she recognized Dana Larson's grin beneath the female mummy's rapidly loosening bandages.

Out of the corner of her eye Elizabeth saw Jessica's Princess Jasmine leap into the arms of a tall, sun-streaked blond Aladdin, and she quickly steered Sue around to one of the refreshment tables. No need to start the fireworks yet.

They got diet sodas and handfuls of chips and stood there watching the crowd surge past.

"Oh, no, look at that." Sue laughed, pointing to a tall, dark Dracula. The vampire leered at them hungrily, then swished his cape and bared his long white fangs.

"Robby!" Elizabeth cried. "You look great."

Robby slunk closer, staring obviously at their necks. "Dahlings," he growled in a foreign accent. "You look de*lic*ious!"

Sue and Elizabeth both laughed, a little nervously. Then Lila came up behind Robby and waved hello.

It took Elizabeth a moment to figure out what Lila's costume was, but when she did, she let out a low whistle. "Lila, that's amazing," she said sincerely. Lila was dressed in a medieval-looking gown of olive-green, with a low neckline. Her hair was parted in the middle and hung in shiny, rippled waves around her shoulders.

Lila turned a little bit, then looked at Elizabeth and gave a small, wistful smile. She held that pose.

"Great, great!" Sue cried, clapping her hands.

Robby put his arm around Lila and held her close. "She's my Mona Lila," he said, kissing her neck. "Isn't she beautiful?"

Lila grinned. "Robby did it all. It's the best costume I've ever had." She beamed up at him; then they drifted away into the crowd, their arms around each other.

"Ugh, they're disgusting," Sue joked.

"They are pretty happy together," Elizabeth agreed. "At least someone is." Her eyes scanned the crowd. So many people had outdone themselves with great outfits. Her recycled black-cat costume felt drab and boring. Elizabeth sighed.

"May I have this dance?" someone asked Sue in an English accent.

Elizabeth laughed when she recognized him. "Winston! Great costume."

Winston grinned and shrugged. "It was the best I could do, given what I had to work with." He ran his hand over his nearly bald head.

Maria came up and hugged him from behind. "Isn't he sexy?" she asked cheerfully.

Winston was wearing a red *Star Trek* uniform, from the new series. His four collar studs and bald head identified him as Captain Picard.

"Almost as sexy as the real Jean-Luc Picard," Sue agreed.

Winston looked outraged. "Almost! What do you mean 'almost'?"

Laughing, Sue took his hand and led him to the dance floor, winking at Maria over Winston's shoulder. They started to dance.

Elizabeth grinned at Maria. "I guess it was either that or the king from *The King and I*."

Maria raised her paper cup in a salute. "You got it, Ensign." Maria herself was dressed as a Vulcan. She had pulled her dark hair back severely and had found pointy ears to go with her own *Star Trek* uniform.

"Elizabeth?" A tall, dark wizard stood in front of them, looking uncertainly into her eyes.

Quickly drawing in a breath, Elizabeth said, "Todd?"

Todd was dressed in black jeans, a shiny purple top, and a long black cape covered with gold stars, moons, and suns. His tall hat was purple and also covered with stars. He took off his hat and looked at Elizabeth.

"You want to dance?" he asked evenly.

Elizabeth stared up at his face, the face that was so familiar, so loved. She had missed him so much and had regretted their stupid argument a thousand times. Then she gasped. "Your mustache!"

Todd grinned. "Yeah, well, I was sick of it. What do you think?" He rubbed a finger over his naked upper lip.

"Oh, it looks *great*," Elizabeth gushed. She peered up at him more closely. "Did you cut your hair, too?"

Todd nodded. "Uh-huh. Just trimmed the top, so

that when it grows out, it'll be more or less the same length. Like it was before."

"Todd, you look so, well, great," Elizabeth said. "You've never looked this handsome before in your life."

Todd gave an embarrassed smile. "So you want to dance?"

"Yes, yes, yes, yes!" Elizabeth said happily. "But first kiss me, please." She stood close to him and rose up on her tiptoes.

"Gladly," Todd said huskily, and he bent down to kiss her mouth.

On the sidelines Maria slapped high five with Winston, who had just come back.

"The little lovebirds," Winston said in a smarmy voice, putting his arms around Maria.

"Where's Sue?" Maria asked him.

"She went to get something to drink. Over there." Winston waved vaguely over by the trees. "Come on. Just one dance with your commanding officer." He tugged her out onto the dance floor.

"Aye, aye, sir," Maria said, giggling.

"Hey, Jess, what's happening?" Lila swerved over to where her friend was sitting on a log bench.

Jessica looked concerned. "Have you seen Jeremy anywhere?"

Lila flopped down beside her, fanning herself with a paper napkin. "Nope," she said. "Maybe Robby will see him by the food table—he went to get us some sandwiches." She smiled happily at Jessica. "Isn't this a great party? I'm having the best time."

"It's good to see you and Robby together again," Jessica said distractedly. "I wish I could say the same about myself."

Then Lila seemed to notice how despondent Jessica was.

"Hey, what's wrong? Jeremy's back, right? So you two are in heaven, aren't you? It's what you've been waiting for for two months." Lila flipped her long brown hair over her shoulder.

Jessica frowned. "That's what I thought too. But I've hardly seen Jeremy since he's been back. And then about ten minutes ago he said he was going to get us something to drink, and I haven't seen him since."

"There's probably a long line," Lila said practically. "Don't get your nylons in a twist."

Jessica looked at Lila impatiently. "It's not just that, Li. It's the whole way he's been acting. Ever since he got back, he's been preoccupied, like I'm not even standing there with him. He's been busy all the time—yesterday I didn't see him at all. I don't know." Jessica's forehead creased in worry. "I just have a bad feeling about this. Like something horrible is about to happen, and I can't stop it."

Lila patted her knee comfortingly. "Look, you're probably still feeling weird because he's been gone for so long. It'll take you guys a few days to get back into the rhythm of things. Just try to relax and have a good time. Everything will be OK." Lila smiled at her reassuringly, but Jessica wasn't convinced.

That's easy for you to say, she thought. *You have Roberino hanging all over you.*

Just then Robby came and lunged toward Lila, playfully biting her neck while she shrieked happily and tried to bat him away. Jessica rolled her eyes and stood up to go look for Jeremy.

"Oh, Todd, this is so nice," Elizabeth breathed, resting her head on his shoulder. She moved gently to the side so that her long black tail would swing out of the way. The Nontoxic Avengers were playing one of the few slow songs in their repertoire, and Elizabeth and Todd were moving together under the Chinese lanterns. The soft night air felt friendly and welcoming, comforting.

"I've missed you," Todd murmured.

"I was so awful," Elizabeth admitted, feeling overwhelmed with guilt.

Todd chuckled against her black-velvet cat hood. "It's amazing you put up with it as long as you did. After I shaved it off, my mom took one look at me and pretended to faint from happiness."

Elizabeth giggled.

"She had really been hating it too but hadn't wanted to put her foot down. She's really glad it's gone, though."

Elizabeth tilted her head back and smiled at him. Now that the hated mustache was gone, she could afford to be generous.

"Maybe in a couple years you can try again." *Like if I'm at a different college a thousand miles away.*

Todd laughed. "Sure."

This really stinks. I'm Jessica Wakefield, not some hapless freshman who can't hang on to a boyfriend.

187

Her teeth gritted, she wove her way through the crowd of dancing party-goers, keeping a lookout for Jeremy's blond head and his shiny blue turban. Suddenly Jessica stopped dead, a horrible thought occurring to her. Winston and Maria, dancing, bumped into her and almost knocked her off her feet.

"Oh, sorry," Jessica muttered, quickly crossing to the other side of the party. *Where is Sue?* That had to be it. Dreary Sue had no doubt grabbed poor Jeremy and dragged him off someplace, and was now bending his ear with a bunch of pitiful whining about how he shouldn't have left her, blah blah blah . . .

Determinedly Jessica scanned the crowd, her eyes narrowed. She had never trusted Sue. All sorts of half memories flooded into Jessica's mind as she threaded her way through the little knots of people standing around, laughing, having a good time. Sue's fake blood disease. Her "suicide" attempt. *I bet that wasn't even real,* Jessica thought cynically. And what about Jeremy? What was going on with him? Not once had he been in his room when Jessica had called—even in the middle of the night. She recalled the fact that he had made her leave the airport before he boarded his plane. *How do I know he even got on the stupid plane?*

Tears of frustration, fear, and anger began to well up in her eyes. What was going on? Why would Sue disappear for hours at a time? Who was that couple in Winston's video, kissing on the beach? Where was Jeremy? Where was he?

Jessica pressed a hand to her eyes, feeling as though she were losing her mind. Half of her thought she was being paranoid, but half of her was screaming that things didn't add up. Things Jeremy had said or done, things Sue had said or done . . .

I have to get out of here. I have to be quiet for a minute. Blindly Jessica left the party and headed toward the wooded area surrounding the cabin. She would just sit under a tree for a few minutes and get a grip. It would be peaceful there, and dark. And if Jeremy was searching for her, if he was getting worried, then so much the better.

Jessica's little slippers strode quietly through the underbrush as she pushed her way into the woods. A few feet in, the sounds and the lights of the party already dimming, Jessica leaned against the rough bark of a tree. One hand to her chest, she stood there, trying to calm her breathing, trying to calm her mind. If she just thought it through, it would all make sense. Everything would fall into place. She just had to think about it.

Some minutes later Jessica felt her head beginning to clear. The night enveloped her, making her feel safe and hidden. She heard the soft cooing of birds settling down for the night, and the rustle of a small animal hurrying toward its burrow. She smiled in the darkness. Her breathing had slowed, and her eyes had adjusted to the woods' faint light. In just another minute she would return to the party. She was sure Jeremy would be waiting there for her, concerned that she had been missing.

Then she heard it. The murmuring of voices, the slithery crush of leaves and bushes as they were pushed aside. There was silence, and then the unmistakable sound of kisses filtered through the trees where Jessica was leaning.

She grinned. Of course the woods would be perfect to steal away with someone special. Who was it? she wondered. Todd and Elizabeth? She grimaced. Lila and Robby? Winston and Maria? Covering her mouth with her hand to smother her laughter, Jessica stood up straighter. She couldn't resist just taking a tiny peek. Then she would have something funny to gossip about in school on Monday.

Very slowly and quietly, her soft shoes making hardly any sound on the damp forest floor, Jessica slipped through the trees toward the sound. A few more feet . . . then she caught a splash of color. Someone's costume standing out in the darkness.

A few more steps took her within eyesight.

For a long moment she stood there, staring. She was dreaming, she had to be dreaming. Soon she would wake up and laugh at the stupidity and cruelty of this dream.

Not ten feet away Jeremy, the love of her life, her dream man, the man she had risked going to boarding school for, was holding another woman, kissing her passionately, pressing her against a tree and holding her head in place so that he could kiss her more deeply. The woman was Sue.

Suddenly they broke apart, and Jeremy wheeled around to face Jessica. She realized belatedly that she must have gasped or made some sound.

"Jessica!" he cried, looking desperately back at Sue. "Darling! It isn't what you think—" He started to head toward her, brushing his blond hair off his face with ragged motions.

"Don't touch me," Jessica stammered through lips as numb as ice.

"Jessica, we weren't doing anything," Sue began, hastily smoothing her witch's cape.

"Save it," Jessica bit out, hot tears flooding her eyes and spilling down over her cheeks. "You two deserve each other." Then she turned and ran headlong back toward the party, toward the lights and people.

"Whoa, Jess," Todd said cheerfully, catching her as she stumbled against a refreshments table. "Hold on there. Don't let that diet Coke go straight to your head like that." Then he saw the glistening tracks of tears down her face, and he straightened up.

"Jessica, what's the matter?" Elizabeth demanded, putting down her plate of food and grabbing her sister's shoulders. She dragged Jessica over by the cabin, away from the noisy crowd.

"It's . . . it's Jeremy," Jessica mumbled, trying to suck back her sobs. She'd rather die than make a huge scene in public, have these people see her cry.

"What? What about him?"

"I saw him," Jessica gasped quietly, trying to keep her voice down. She turned her back to the party so no one could see her tormented face. "Liz—he and Sue were in the woods, making out. Together. They were totally kissing. I saw them!" She broke down in sobs again.

Todd swore softly under his breath. "That jerk. I'm going to go find him—"

Elizabeth put a hand on his arm. "Hold on. Jess, what do you mean? You're sure you saw them?"

"I was ten feet away!" Jessica cried miserably. "Don't you see? He was just using me! He wants Sue, after all. He wants her money." Tears ran down her face and dripped off her chin, and she dashed them angrily away.

"But she doesn't get the money now," Elizabeth said slowly, staring into Jessica's eyes. "It hasn't been two months yet."

"Oh, Liz!" Jessica snapped. "It doesn't matter. I don't know why they're together, but they are. It looked like he was giving her a tonsillectomy! Come on—I have to get out of here. Give me the keys to the Jeep." She held out her hand. It was shaking.

"No, Jess. You're too upset to drive. I'll take you. One second."

Elizabeth turned to Todd, an apologetic look on her face. "I'm sorry. I really have to take her home."

Todd squeezed her hand. "It's OK. I'll probably go home soon myself. It won't be any fun without you here." He gazed lovingly into her eyes.

"Could we hurry it up here? My heart is bleeding all over the ground," Jessica snarled, practically choking through her sobs.

"OK, OK." Quickly giving Todd a last kiss, Elizabeth took Jessica's arm and they hurried out to the parking area.

Just as Elizabeth was starting the Jeep and pulling out, Jeremy ran up beside them, panting from running.

"Honey! Wait a minute! Can't we talk?"

"I don't want to talk to you." Jessica sobbed, covering her face.

"Liz, help me out here," Jeremy pleaded.

Elizabeth couldn't believe his nerve. "I wouldn't help you if you were falling off a cliff," she snapped. "Now, take a hike, you two-timing jerk, before I run you over!"

Jeremy's dark eyes widened, and he looked from Jessica back to Elizabeth, as though he couldn't believe they were both so willing to leave him behind.

With a final narrow-eyed glare, Elizabeth pulled the Jeep quickly out of the parking lot, looking back in satisfaction to see gravel spraying all over Jeremy.

Back at the Wakefields', Elizabeth made two cups of steaming hot chocolate and a buttery bowl of popcorn in a not-very-successful effort to comfort her weeping sister.

"I should have seen it, Liz," Jessica kept saying through her tears. "I'm so stupid. Why didn't I see it? They were lying to me all the time."

Elizabeth wasn't sure about that, but she did know that she was going to hit Sue with some questions when she got home. *But what can I say?* Elizabeth thought wryly, as she brought the hot chocolate to the table. *"How dare you steal your fiancé back from my sister, who stole him from you in the first place?"* she thought, sighing. *Why either one of them wants that two-timing creep is beyond me.*

Elizabeth handed the cocoa to her sister as she sat down. "Here, drink some of this," she coaxed, "it will make you feel better."

"I'll never feel better," declared Jessica dramatically, cupping the steaming mug in her hands. Fresh tears clouded her eyes and trickled down her face into the hot chocolate. "How could he do this to me? How could he betray me like—hey, what's that?" Jessica asked, sitting up suddenly.

As Elizabeth listened to the usual night sounds of the Wakefield household, she could hear a faint knocking on the front door. Jessica's eyes lit up with hope.

Oh, no! Elizabeth thought in alarm, overcome with a protective feeling for her love-struck sister. If it was Jeremy, she wasn't going to let him sweet-talk Jessica into forgiving him. "Don't worry, I'll take care of it," Elizabeth assured her, jumping up.

If that two-timing louse has the nerve to show up here now, I am going to give him a piece of my mind, thought Elizabeth as she marched resolutely into the foyer. Maybe Jessica's actions hadn't been particularly admirable lately, but all the same—nobody got away with cheating on her twin sister.

Elizabeth peered through the peephole of the solid front door, and sure enough, there was the rat himself. She flung the door open and fixed Jeremy with a steely stare. "If you're here to make excuses to my sister, you can just forget it, because she's had it with you!" proclaimed Elizabeth in her haughtiest tone. As Jeremy opened his mouth to respond, Elizabeth slammed the door in his face.

"No, wait!" Jessica called from the kitchen, scrambling out of her chair and careening around the corner.

Jeremy knocked again, and Jessica gave her sister a reproving look and pulled the door open. The sight of Jeremy's chiseled face surrounded by a halo of golden hair made her melt. For a moment, she didn't care that she had just caught Jeremy with Sue.

She gazed up into his eyes, prepared to run into his arms. But suddenly she registered a look on his face that she had never seen before: fear.

"It's Sue," Jeremy said, his face ashen. "She's disappeared."

What's happened to Sue Gibbons? Find out the shocking truth in Sweet Valley High #110, **Death Threat**, *the second book in this spellbinding three-part miniseries.*

Bantam Books in the Sweet Valley High series
Ask your bookseller for the books you have missed

#1 DOUBLE LOVE
#2 SECRETS
#3 PLAYING WITH FIRE
#4 POWER PLAY
#5 ALL NIGHT LONG
#6 DANGEROUS LOVE
#7 DEAR SISTER
#8 HEARTBREAKER
#9 RACING HEARTS
#10 WRONG KIND OF GIRL
#11 TOO GOOD TO BE TRUE
#12 WHEN LOVE DIES
#13 KIDNAPPED!
#14 DECEPTIONS
#15 PROMISES
#16 RAGS TO RICHES
#17 LOVE LETTERS
#18 HEAD OVER HEELS
#19 SHOWDOWN
#20 CRASH LANDING!
#21 RUNAWAY
#22 TOO MUCH IN LOVE
#23 SAY GOODBYE
#24 MEMORIES
#25 NOWHERE TO RUN
#26 HOSTAGE
#27 LOVESTRUCK
#28 ALONE IN THE CROWD
#29 BITTER RIVALS
#30 JEALOUS LIES
#31 TAKING SIDES
#32 THE NEW JESSICA
#33 STARTING OVER
#34 FORBIDDEN LOVE
#35 OUT OF CONTROL
#36 LAST CHANCE
#37 RUMORS
#38 LEAVING HOME
#39 SECRET ADMIRER
#40 ON THE EDGE

#41 OUTCAST
#42 CAUGHT IN THE MIDDLE
#43 HARD CHOICES
#44 PRETENSES
#45 FAMILY SECRETS
#46 DECISIONS
#47 TROUBLEMAKER
#48 SLAM BOOK FEVER
#49 PLAYING FOR KEEPS
#50 OUT OF REACH
#51 AGAINST THE ODDS
#52 WHITE LIES
#53 SECOND CHANCE
#54 TWO-BOY WEEKEND
#55 PERFECT SHOT
#56 LOST AT SEA
#57 TEACHER CRUSH
#58 BROKENHEARTED
#59 IN LOVE AGAIN
#60 THAT FATAL NIGHT
#61 BOY TROUBLE
#62 WHO'S WHO?
#63 THE NEW ELIZABETH
#64 THE GHOST OF TRICIA MARTIN
#65 TROUBLE AT HOME
#66 WHO'S TO BLAME?
#67 THE PARENT PLOT
#68 THE LOVE BET
#69 FRIEND AGAINST FRIEND
#70 MS. QUARTERBACK
#71 STARRING JESSICA!
#72 ROCK STAR'S GIRL
#73 REGINA'S LEGACY
#74 THE PERFECT GIRL
#75 AMY'S TRUE LOVE
#76 MISS TEEN SWEET VALLEY
#77 CHEATING TO WIN
#78 THE DATING GAME
#79 THE LONG-LOST BROTHER

#80 THE GIRL THEY BOTH LOVED

#81 ROSA'S LIE

#82 KIDNAPPED BY THE CULT!

#83 STEVEN'S BRIDE

#84 THE STOLEN DIARY

#85 SOAP STAR

#86 JESSICA AGAINST BRUCE

#87 MY BEST FRIEND'S BOYFRIEND

#88 LOVE LETTERS FOR SALE

#89 ELIZABETH BETRAYED

#90 DON'T GO HOME WITH JOHN

#91 IN LOVE WITH A PRINCE

#92 SHE'S NOT WHAT SHE SEEMS

#93 STEPSISTERS

#94 ARE WE IN LOVE?

#95 THE MORNING AFTER

#96 THE ARREST

#97 THE VERDICT

#98 THE WEDDING

#99 BEWARE THE BABY-SITTER

#100 THE EVIL TWIN (MAGNA)

#101 THE BOYFRIEND WAR

#102 ALMOST MARRIED

#103 OPERATION LOVE MATCH

#104 LOVE AND DEATH IN LONDON

#105 A DATE WITH A WEREWOLF

#106 BEWARE THE WOLFMAN (SUPER THRILLER)

#107 JESSICA'S SECRET LOVE

#108 LEFT AT THE ALTAR

#109 DOUBLE-CROSSED

SUPER EDITIONS:
PERFECT SUMMER
SPECIAL CHRISTMAS
SPRING BREAK
MALIBU SUMMER
WINTER CARNIVAL
SPRING FEVER

SUPER STARS:
LILA'S STORY
BRUCE'S STORY
ENID'S STORY
OLIVIA'S STORY
TODD'S STORY

SUPER THRILLERS:
DOUBLE JEOPARDY
ON THE RUN
NO PLACE TO HIDE
DEADLY SUMMER
MURDER ON THE LINE
BEWARE THE WOLFMAN

MAGNA EDITIONS:
THE WAKEFIELDS OF SWEET VALLEY
THE WAKEFIELD LEGACY: THE UNTOLD STORY
A NIGHT TO REMEMBER
THE EVIL TWIN
ELIZABETH'S SECRET DIARY
JESSICA'S SECRET DIARY

SIGN UP FOR THE SWEET VALLEY HIGH® FAN CLUB!

Hey, girls! Get all the gossip on Sweet Valley High's® most popular teenagers when you join our fantastic Fan Club! As a member, you'll get all of this really cool stuff:

- Membership Card with your own personal Fan Club ID number
- A Sweet Valley High® Secret Treasure Box
- Sweet Valley High® Stationery
- Official Fan Club Pencil (for secret note writing!)
- Three Bookmarks
- A "Members Only" Door Hanger
- Two Skeins of J. & P. Coats® Embroidery Floss with flower barrette instruction leaflet
- Two editions of *The Oracle* newsletter
- Plus exclusive Sweet Valley High® product offers, special savings, contests, and much more!

Be the first to find out what Jessica & Elizabeth Wakefield are up to by joining the Sweet Valley High® Fan Club for the one-year membership fee of only $6.25 each for U.S. residents, $8.25 for Canadian residents (U.S. currency). Includes shipping & handling.

Send a check or money order (do not send cash) made payable to "Sweet Valley High® Fan Club" along with this form to:

SWEET VALLEY HIGH® FAN CLUB, BOX 3919-B, SCHAUMBURG, IL 60168-3919

NAME_____
(Please print clearly)

ADDRESS_____

CITY_____ STATE _____ ZIP_____
(Required)

AGE_____ BIRTHDAY_____ /_____ /_____

Your friends at Sweet Valley High have had their world turned upside down!

Meet one person with a power so evil, so dangerous, that it could destroy the entire world of Sweet Valley!

A Night to Remember, the book that starts it all, is followed by a six book series filled with romance, drama and suspense.

Life after high school gets even *Sweeter!*

Jessica and Elizabeth are now freshmen at Sweet Valley University, where the motto is: Welcome to college — welcome to freedom!

Don't miss any of the books in this fabulous new series.

♥ College Girls #1   0-553-56308-4 $3.50/$4.50 Can.

♥ Love, Lies and
  Jessica Wakefield #2   0-553-56306-8 $3.50/$4.50 Can.

♥ What Your Parents
  Don't Know #3   0-553-56307-6 $3.50/$4.50 Can.

♥ Anything for Love #4   0-553-56311-4 $3.50/$4.50 Can.

♥ A Married Woman #5   0-553-56309-2 $3.50/$4.50 Can.

♥ The Love of Her Life #6   0-553-56310-6 $3.50/$4.50 Can.

Bantam Doubleday Dell
Books for Young Readers

Bantam Doubleday Dell
Dept. SVU 12
2451 South Wolf Road
Des Plaines, IL 60018

Please send the items I have checked above. I am enclosing $_____$ (please add $2.50 to cover postage and handling). Send check or money order, no cash or C.O.D.s please.

Name

Address

City   State   Zip

Please allow four to six weeks for delivery.
Prices and availability subject to change without notice.   **SVU 12 4/94**